the

end

of

me

john gould

the
end
of
me

Freehand Books acknowledges the financial support for its publishing program provided by the Canada Council for the Arts and the Alberta Media Fund, and by the Government of Canada through the Canada Book Fund.

Freehand Books
515 – 815 1st Street SW   Calgary, Alberta   T2P 1N3
www.freehand-books.com

Book orders: UTP Distribution
5201 Dufferin Street Toronto, Ontario   M3H 5T8
Telephone: 1-800-565-9523   Fax: 1-800-221-9985
utpbooks@utpress.utoronto.ca utpdistribution.com

Library and Archives Canada Cataloguing in Publication
Title: The end of me / John Gould.
Names: Gould, John, 1959– author.
Description: Short stories.
Identifiers: Canadiana (print) 20190213914 | Canadiana (ebook) 20190213949
ISBN 9781988298566 (softcover) | ISBN 9781988298573 (EPUB)
ISBN 9781988298580 (PDF)
Classification: LCC PS8563.O8446 E53 2020 | DDC C813/.54—dc23

Edited by Deborah Willis
Book design by Natalie Olsen, Kisscut Design
Author photo by Sandy Mayzel
Printed on FSC® recycled paper and bound in Canada by Marquis

For Sandy

After your death you will be what you were
before your birth.
ARTHUR SCHOPENHAUER, thinking

There is absolutely no other free act granted to us,
only the destruction of the "I."
SIMONE WEIL, praying

I don't understand what I'm supposed to do.
LEO TOLSTOY, dying

contents

Dreams of Love

As soon as the funeral director, Lawrence-call-me-Larry, stepped out of his office, the phone began to ring. Renée, who sat with her brother's cremated remains on her lap, glanced over at her sister Chris, who glanced back. They were both having the same thought, which was that Zack, if he still existed, would have picked up the phone. What would he have said?

"Remember?" said Renée.

Chris nodded. She was thinking of the time, back when they were kids, Zack called a random number and convinced the woman who answered that Jesus had returned and needed someplace to crash. The woman offered up her guest room, which Zack declined because it was in the basement and, as the woman confessed, "not airy," a phrase which became code amongst the three of them for anything that disappointed. Renée, on the other hand, was thinking of the

time Zack took a call from a telemarketer and set about con-
verting him to Eckankar, a religion he'd just read about in
line at the grocery store, actually getting the guy to close his
eyes and guide his soul back towards its source. If either of
the sisters had known they were recalling different (though
thematically related) incidents, it would have made them even
bluer than they already were.

The phone stopped ringing. Renée hefted the box in her
lap. The box was actually a birdhouse Zack had built during
his carpentry phase, the little round door sealed off now to
prevent his ashes spilling out. Some weeks ago the women had
lined up babysitters and spent an afternoon searching for the
perfect container, lugging with them a bag of orzo to stand in
for Zack's remains. Research had helped them estimate him
at twelve cups – he was alive and on a modest upswing at the
time – though this proved generous. They chipped in on three
different vessels that day, none of them quite right. Back at
Chris's place they shared a bottle of Malbec and gazed out
on her tiny backyard, where the birdhouse hung unoccupied,
between families. Between families – that was Zack's condition too, since he'd left their family, his first one, and never
settled into a second.

Lawrence-call-me-Larry popped his head back into the
office. "Sorry, bit of trouble with the printer." He required the
women to sign a waiver confirming that it wasn't the funeral
home's responsibility if Zack's ashes escaped the nonstan-
dard receptacle into which he'd just placed them. It was in
search of this paperwork that he'd set out. At his reappear-
ance, Renée and Chris shared a glance which said, *Weird how*

robust this guy is, how animated, when what he deals with all day is dead people. Or maybe not so weird.

"No worries," said Renée.

Lawrence-call-me-Larry disappeared again. Almost instantly the phone resumed ringing. The sisters exchanged another glance.

"You," said Chris.

"You," said Renée.

"Acme Morgue here," said Chris. "You stab 'em, we slab 'em."

"You kill 'em, we chill 'em."

"You ghost 'em, we roast 'em."

With this, the women ran out of lines recollected from the days they'd all three still lived at home, and Zack had amused himself goading his little sisters into mischief. Chris went back to wondering how to work the phrase "not airy" into her part of the eulogy in such a way as to convey its special meaning without having to recite the whole story. Renée went back to wondering why the eulogy and indeed all these arrangements had been left to the two of them, their parents having gone useless in the aftermath of Zack's death. How was one to judge or even comprehend another's grief?

The phone continued to ring. Its ringtone was a horribly synthesized version of the famous somber bit from Franz Liszt's *Liebesträum*, a title either of them could have produced but which only Zack, if he were present, could have translated from the German as *Dreams of Love*.

Both women reached a decision at the same moment. Chris was closer to the phone, so she was the one who snatched it up. "Hello?" she said. Anticlimactic, but a start, she figured. The thing was to take action, just as Zack would have done, trusting inspiration to arise from the moment.

Dial tone – the caller had hung up. "Yes, that's right," Chris said into the phone. "How can we help you in your time of need?" She made a what-have-I-got-myself-into face at Renée.

Renée made a you-go-girl face back.

"Yes, of course," said Chris into the phone, "we'll come right away and collect ... Albert, is it? We would like you to consider, though, that Albert may already be elsewhere. Or nowhere. That is to say, what we collect may not be Albert."

Renée raised her eyebrows, wow. She also raised the bird-house, briefly, and set it back down again.

Chris shrugged. "But Jesus," she said, "and the Buddha and so on, aren't they all saying the same thing, way down deep?" She paused and listened intently. "No, deeper than that." She paused again. "Deeper." Another pause. "Well, that nothing is the nothing of the nothing."

She grimaced at Renée, who gave her a thumbs up.

"Uh-huh," said Chris into the phone. "Uh-huh ... Well, that's a great question. And there are a lot of other great questions too. Such as ..." She flashed Renée a panicky look.

Renée whispered, *"Who's a good dog?"*

"Who's a good dog?" said Chris into the phone.

"Are we there yet?"

"Are we there yet?"

"Do you know the muffin man?"

"Do you know the muffin man?"

No question, Zack was there in the room with them, present in what passed between his sisters. He was also absent, of course, and in this way too he was present. This was precisely his style, after all, to get himself strung out between two true things that couldn't both be.

Renée whispered, *"What shall we do with a drunken sailor?"*

"What shall we do with a drunken sailor?" said Chris into the phone.

Renée reached out her hand.

Chris took it.

"Who knew?"

"Who knew?"

Surge

What you're supposed to do with your life is get ready to die, or anyway that's what the dead guys you read in first year say, and also your girlfriend's sister's creepy guru if your girlfriend is Cassie, which mine is. I'm pretty sure. The basic thing being to get so far past your own selfness that when you die it's no big deal because it's already happened, you've let stuff go. But to be honest I don't have that kind of time. The ball cancer (my therapist says go ahead and call it that, and so does my gynecologist which is what I call my oncologist just to mess with her), so yeah, the ball cancer has spread, it's not just in my left ball anymore but all over the place. Including my brain, so I wouldn't necessarily buy any of this. Besides which, I haven't a clue what death is, so how would I get ready for it? The whole selfnessless thing, what if that isn't even the point? How can a guru that creepy be right about stuff?

Like I say, it's mostly that I don't have the time, or the energy either. Just tapping this out I have to take a nap after every other sentence practically, which is pretty fricking good for me these days, to tell you the truth. So what I'm getting ready for isn't my death but my Final Surge of Energy, which is actually an actual medical thing. A couple of days or even hours before you croak (my therapist says go ahead and call it that, just be real about stuff) the tiredness is suddenly sucked out of you and you fill up with whatever you used to be full of. They think it might be your brain gushing out all its chemicals before it quits, and suddenly you can talk if you haven't been talking or tear into a good meal if you haven't been eating or whatever.

Here's how I imagine it. You're at a party or a bar or something but you're totally bummed because the girl you like (Cassie, in my case) isn't there and your friend smoked the weed he was supposed to share with you and the spiced rums you had at home to save a few bucks aren't giving you any sort of buzz at all, and you figure you'll sit in the corner and glare at all the other pathetic morons for the rest of the night or maybe go down to 7-Eleven and buy a dozen Ho Hos and head home to crash on the couch in front of the *Doctor Who* marathon. But suddenly your song comes on, the one with the amazing bass line, and the rum kicks in and Cassie shows up and grabs you by the arm and pulls you out into the middle of everything and you're jumping around and spinning like a little kid or like one of those dervish guys who do it to get close to God. The difference being that when the dance is over you're gone, poof.

I hate dancing, plus why would that be the thing to do with your Final Surge of Energy? I put it out on Faceplant to get some ideas, even though that's usually depressing. People said things like I'd get up early and watch the sun rise or I'd write a letter to all the special people in my life or I'd finally forgive myself or I'd go downtown and hug strangers and tell them life is precious or I'd rob a bank or steal a pony from the petting zoo or freebase cocaine and hump till my heart stopped or whatever. A lot of people said we should live like that all the time, like each moment is our last, and I almost but didn't quite tell them it won't work. I mean sure, go ahead and try to convince yourself your life could be over any moment, but you won't believe it, not till one of your balls is gone and you can't sit up without fainting or eat without heaving. Try to imagine this, go ahead. You'll think you are but you aren't.

Almost anybody with kids said that's what they'd spend their Final Surge on, is their kids, which gave me my idea. I still have my right ball and there's no cancer in it, in fact my gynecologist says it's super-powered, cranking out extra juice to make up for the one they cut off. Plus I haven't had radiation in weeks and I've managed to get off a couple of times, so the new sperm in there should be good to go. I haven't told Cassie, even though she's been here three times this week, and one time she gave me a little tongue when she kissed me goodbye which she's not supposed to do because I have no immune system but screw it. Actually, I did tell her about the Surge. She cried, which is about the hottest thing in the universe, a girl crying for you, and I got a bit of a boner which doesn't sound like a big deal but it is. But I didn't tell her what I'm hoping to do with my Surge. It has to be spontaneous. Either she'll go with it or she won't. When the Surge hits I'll get up and go find her and we'll see.

Maybe I'll put it out on Faceplant. Hey girls, if a guy came up and asked can I knock you up just before I die, it's my only chance to live on, what would you say? Though when I put it like that it sounds kind of douchey. Maybe the whole idea is a bad one, maybe it's not what I should do with my Surge. Maybe you shouldn't decide what to do with your Surge till you're Surging anyway, just let the energy tell you how to spend it. Like when you're born you start screaming and then you start sucking, not because you planned it that way but

Metal

Back from band practice, Joni says, "Whatcha reading, Mum?"

It's one in the morning, way late for a school night, but I decide to leave that be. "Nothing much," I say, because the book's a piece of fluff, and anyway I'm not reading it. Joni frets if she knows I'm fretting, or at least she used to, so I keep something handy I can pretend to concentrate on. I miss the days I actually could concentrate, maybe get through a magazine article, but there you go.

Joni doesn't care, she just wants to talk. "How was practice?" I ask her.

"Okay. We got the gig."

"Joni! That's wonderful."

"I guess."

"You guess?"

She slams herself into the other easy chair. She's fully decked out tonight — Derk likes to snark that she could be "a crack ho turning tricks in a crypt," missing the point that this is exactly the look she's going for. The top she's got on tonight gouges particularly low, so you can see the goat head and most of the androgynous body of Baphomet, the beast she's recently had tattooed onto her left breast by Spike, her guy down at Tribal. The skin around the image is still red but not, I note, oozy. Maybe she's using the ointment I gave her.

"Now we need a band name," she says.

"Ah. And you can't agree on one."

"That."

What's going on here is that Joni wants everything to be communal, collective. She refuses to impose her will on the other girls, even though she's the one who writes and sings all the songs. She got the musical thing from me (I named her after Joni Mitchell), and she got the fanatical fair-mindedness from me too, I'm afraid.

I ask her, "What name does Deanna like?" Deanna's the drummer. She's generally on the other side of any rift in the band.

"Carcass." Joni fidgets with the thick metal ring that runs through her septum, in one nostril and out the other.

"Hm, not bad," I say. "But you like …?"

"Mary Magdalene's Twat."

"I see. A bit … funnier? More sophisticated?"

"Sure, I guess."

This is a big deal for Joni. It's her chance to make a mark, make a statement about who she is as a creative individual. She's done a demo on her laptop, and she's been pushing hard to get this gig at an outdoor festival, which happens to be dry, so their being underage isn't a problem. Derk would love the band to break up, or at least lose the gig (which they're pretty sure to do if they go with the word "twat"), and of course I'd love it too if Joni would go back to viola in the school orchestra and start eating and sleeping and speaking to people again, but I'll never help my daughter fail. Not ever. Derk can go to hell.

Which isn't fair. He adores her, of course he does, and he's scared (though he can't possibly be as scared as I am), but what he doesn't get is the innocence of it all. When Joni sings *Death did me like a dog last night* she could just as well be singing *Jimmy kissed me on the lips last night.* It'd mean the same thing to her, pretty much. She has no idea about these things, she can't have or she wouldn't be able to say the words. It's art, it's artifice. *Gangbanged by the ghosts of what we've ruined* – she's a poet, is what she is.

"How's your voice holding up?" I say.

"It's fine, Mum."

This is a worry for me, a trivial enough one that I can say it out loud. Joni's got a lovely voice, but what she does for the band is a sort of guttural roar. She has to sound like that or the band won't be taken seriously as death metal – it's incredible how fussy and elitist some of these little drips can be. My brother used to be able to say "cruisin' for a bruisin'" with one burp, and that's kind of what this is, belching more than singing. What will it do to her vocal chords?

She can see I'm still unsure. "Really, my voice is fine," she says, and impromptu she gives me the first few bars of "Blue," my favourite Joni Mitchell song.

It's beautiful. It's so beautiful I could burst, I could die, but I don't. I don't even cry. "Pretty Dead?" I say.

"What?"

"For your band name. You're all pretty, so Pretty Dead?"

"Colleen's not pretty."

"Oh. I suppose not. Okay, but you're all good kids. Good and Dead?"

"Meh."

"Or hey, how about just Dead Girls? Keep it simple. An all-girl death metal band – Dead Girls."

Joni gets a look. "Mum, nice one. Dead Girls. Dead Girls. Dead Girls."

And then I do start to cry, and I have to come up with a reason. "Your grandma," I say. "She'd have been so proud." My mum died a year ago, in gentler times, back when Joni was still into plain old thrash metal, and had one steady boyfriend and maybe three piercings in her face. Mum might have called it "a mercy," a favourite expression of hers. As in, it's a mercy you're burping instead of singing so people can't make out what you want to say to them.

Joni stretches out and gives me a little shove with her bare foot, an act of great intimacy for her these days. "I miss her," she says.

"Me too."

"Do you think she's ...?"

"Do I think she's what, honey? Still around in some way?"

"Still mad at me."

"Mad? Why on earth?"

Joni shrugs. "Just everything. We need a band photo too, for the gig. Can I borrow your big camera?"

"Sure. But —"

"Or would you maybe even shoot it for us?"

"Joni. I'd love to."

She halfway smiles. "We're gonna do it on the church steps."

"Sounds good."

"And we'll have, like, crowns of thorns. Except barbed wire. Viv's making them."

"Right."

"And we'll be dry-humping our instruments."

"Uh-huh."

She peers at me again, still not convinced. "You're okay with all this?"

"Of course, honey. Absolutely."

Faithful

The last time I ever saw him, my dad made a confession to me. He'd just had his bath, and was sitting on the edge of the tub while I patted him dry. It was an intricate business – he'd lost almost half his weight over the last couple of years, so that his skin was now rumpled up like a hairless cat's.

"Ouch," he said, though I couldn't possibly have hurt him. "There's something I need to say to you."

"That's okay, Dad. Let's just get you into your jammies."

"I'm not … I haven't always been a good man," he said.

"Me neither. Other leg." I was speaking to him the way Tanya would have been doing if it weren't her Friday night off. Tender but taking no guff. Not us at all.

"A faithful man," Dad went on. He took his big bald head in his hands and gave it a squeeze, a gesture he'd recently improvised. "I wasn't always … I failed to be faithful." His eyes went wide at this turn of phrase. "I failed to be faithful, Son. To your mother."

I gripped him under the arms, hoisted him to his feet. My bad shoulder gave me an irritable ping. No, it was my good shoulder. Bloody hell. "Ups-a-daisy," I said. I steadied him, knelt to pull up his bottoms.

"Her name was ... her name was Lorna." He choked off a little gasp of grief.

"That's okay, Dad." I pulled his drawstring tight around his waist – everything was giant on him now, even the nearly-new stuff – and tied it in a bow. "It's all okay. Arm."

He stuck it out and stared at it mistrustfully. "She got pregnant. Lorna. A little girl. You ..." He paused, working it out. "You have a sister. You have a half sister. You've never met her. *I've* never met her."

"Dad –"

"A woman by now."

This was new, the sister. Most times Dad made his confession, Lorna – she was sometimes Linda – terminated the pregnancy. If she gave birth, the baby never made it.

There were other differences too. There were always new developments when Dad revisited his tale – willful fudgings, no doubt, in concert with a faulty memory – but on this occasion they were particularly dramatic. In most versions the affair lasted months, for instance, but in this one it was years. In most versions Dad and the woman agreed to end it, but in this one he broke things off himself. And then the kicker.

"It was you," he said.

"What? Pardon?" I'd given up trying to get him into his bathrobe, and simply maneuvered him over to his recliner. If he got cold I could always crank up the heat. It was time for his nightly read. Of late Dad had reverted to kids' books, not books from his own childhood but from mine – the books he'd read to me, or might conceivably have read if he hadn't been out on the road most of the time, providing. Mum had given the books their own shelf in the living room when I moved out, and after she died, many years later, Dad took an interest in them. He wasn't capable of keeping track of a story any longer, but he seemed to enjoy the sentences, the shape of certain scenes. We'd been through *The Hobbit*, a whole stack of *The Hardy Boys*. His eyes were poor, so it was Tanya or I who did the reading, perched on a little stool next to his big chair. Dad and I were on the *Narnia* series now, near the end of book three, where the lamb turns into a lion and tells the brother and sister to return to their own world and search for him there. The lion stood for Jesus, as Dad had taken to reminding me. Tanya's influence. I kept meaning to speak to her about it.

"It was because of you," said Dad. "That's why I didn't leave. For Lorna. She wanted ... But you."

This was the most distressing new twist to Dad's story, distressing in part because it demonstrated how resolutely blind I'd been of late. Dad might actually have bailed on us, walked out on Mum and me back when I was a boy. How had I failed to acknowledge this? Dad had been breaking the news of his infidelity to me every week for the last few months, yet it had never dawned on me that our family had been in danger. I'd somehow assumed that his regret, the regret he expressed each and every time he tore the tale out of himself, was for having strayed. Now it struck me – it was mostly my dark mood, I think – that what he really regretted was sticking around.

I opened our book – *The Voyage of the Dawn Treader*, a too-lovely title – and closed it again. "Was that a mistake?" I said. "Letting her go?"

Dad stared at me, startled.

"And why are you telling me this now?" Another question that suddenly felt urgent. Why had it not felt that way before? The first night Dad confessed to me I'd been shocked stupid, and I guess I'd never quite snapped out of it. What he most wanted me to believe on that occasion was that my mother never knew. And I did believe it. Mum had become touchingly frank near the end of her life, and wouldn't have kept such a traumatic bit of history to herself. As far as I could recall there'd been no particular Lorna or Linda in their lives. Dad's mistress would have been somebody he ran into on his sales circuit, a ladies'-wear buyer or shop girl looking to be bamboozled by a big galoot from elsewhere.

I didn't challenge Dad that first night, press him with any questions. My goal was to reassure him, keep him calm, and I stuck to that approach with each repetition of the scene. The prospect of Dad getting hysterical was more ghastly than anything I could imagine him dredging up from the past.

"The lion is Jesus," Dad said. He'd worked his way forward on his recliner, and was pointing at the illustration on the cover of the book in my lap.

"Yes, Dad, I know." How was it possible he remembered this, and not the name of my ex-wife, or, many days, the name of my son, his own grandson? How was it possible he remembered he had something to confess and not that he'd already confessed it?

I fished out my reading glasses, turned to our page. "Maybe you should have gone, Dad. Maybe you'd have been happier with her." I was finally accepting that I could say anything to him. He'd almost certainly forget it. What I forgot was that I wouldn't. "We can say whatever we like to one another, right? Make up stories? Make them up again next time? Lulu and I are getting back together, Dad. Lulu, my wife?"

"Lulu," he said, nodding gamely. "Wonderful."

"And Caleb's back in school."

"How about that."

"Caleb? My son?"

"Of course." Some conviction here.

"What was your daughter's name, Dad? Did you give her one? Did Lorna? Maybe we could look her up."

It went on like this for a while, me spewing all sorts of bitter nonsense, Dad doing his best to make it a conversation. Eventually I just ran out of material to riff on, and took up the book again. We were almost finished. The children returned to their world through a door in the sky, left and stayed gone.

❦

Wayner110

For his profile on UniT, Wayne had put "long walks in the woods," more beguiling he figured than "binge drinking" or "crying jags." So here he was in his brand new hiking boots, which he'd vigorously defiled in the muddy lane around back of his apartment building, pretending at first and then actually being a little blissed out by all the nature. There were leaves through which a warmish wind blew, and amongst which birds hopped and twittered. And there was Lara72 (he was sticking with her online name, though she didn't seem to find this quite as charmingly nutty as he'd hoped she might), a bit of wildlife too he supposed, in her leggings and almost peasant blouse. Everything she wore was some shade of purple, which presumably said something about her, but what? Holly had been more golds and browns, but Holly (and her new guy Hank) was exactly what not to think about right now.

"The store's just my day job," Lara72 was saying. "I teach yoga out of my house. That's what I really love." She was precisely the right amount of pretty, from Wayne's point of view, and she was maybe good or something. Warm in a deeply unselfconscious way. The yoga thing was intriguing, but scary. Wouldn't she expect him, too, to be peaceful and fit? This was his first date in however long. His plan had been not to care, but he did. He already did.

"Yoga, eh?" he said. He sought to strike a pose he'd seen on a yoga poster – they were everywhere these days – in which you went into a deep knee bend with your legs out wide and raised your hands as though to surrender. But the position was impossible to hold, plus it put him in mind of those Maori man-dances you saw in anything about New Zealand. Going with it, he set about stamping his feet and slapping his body, also managing the grunts and the big eyes and the lizardy tongue. He kept at this until Lara72 gave him a hesitant half-laugh, the kind of laugh you bestow on an offensive joke told by somebody of whom you want to keep thinking well.

"No, just kidding," he said. "Yeah, yoga." He nodded as though to acknowledge an insight at which they'd arrived after much mutual soul-searching.

Lara72 led the way on down the cedar-chipped path. "What about you, Wayne? What do you ...?"

Indeed, thought Wayne. What do I? "Oh, a little of this and a little ... Actually, I'm learning to cook."

Until this moment, Wayne had thought of his new hobby as a capitulation – to singleness, to the need to be, probably forever, self-sufficient. With Holly he'd been the attentive helper. He'd chopped, stirred, scrubbed, but he'd never taken the lead. It was only because he was alone now that he'd consented to learn a little. Was there a chance, though, that he'd inadvertently made himself interesting?

Lara72 wasn't looking bored, exactly, so he plowed on. "It's like some kind of, I don't know, alchemy?" he said. "You put these different ingredients together, and ..." He did a thing with his hands meant to evoke a merging and transcendence.

"Like yoga!" said Lara72. "Which means yoke, the word yoga. So union." She gestured at the world around her, the chaotic woods and also an elderly couple striding past with those ski poles serious walkers were suddenly using. "Body and mind but also, you know, yourself and everything else."

"Exactly," said Wayne.

Lara72 reached out and plucked a leaf from his hair — a few trees were already autumn-red and shedding. Wayne startled, but recovered with a self-deprecating smirk.

"What's your specialty?" she said.

"Oh, I don't know." Mango margaritas? "My parmesan sage pork chops usually turn out okay."

"Yum," said Lara72. "You're making me hungry."

A minor miracle, this. She did yoga. Shouldn't she be vegetarian? Vegan? "I'm going to learn how to forage, too," said Wayne. He peered about. "None of this looks like food, right? But I mean, people have lived here for thousands of years. It's probably *all* food."

Perhaps because this was his last thought before the raccoon appeared, Wayne first saw it as quarry. If he'd had a spear he would have slung it. Almost immediately, though, it became clear that the raccoon had already been wounded in some way. Half its body, the right half, was malfunctioning, so that as it ran it skidded along the ground in a clockwise arc. It crossed the path and crashed into the woods, reappearing another twenty feet on. It completed this circle twice more before either of them spoke.

"A car," said Lara72.

Indeed, Wayne was aware now that he'd been hearing traffic all along. They hadn't left civilization so far behind after all. "Crud," he said.

"Poor thing."

Well, he'd have to kill it. You couldn't let a fellow sentient being suffer, not on a first date. And if there was killing to be done, surely that duty fell to the man. There was no way to be certain he'd be doing the creature a favour – running around in painful circles might turn out to be far better than being dead – but you couldn't risk saying that. *What if there's a hell? What if the Babylonians were right, or maybe it was the Mesopotamians, what if we're all going to spend the rest of forever in the dark eating dust?* Not a suave rejoinder, no. There were so many things you were better off keeping to yourself.

Wayne stooped and picked up a rock from the edge of the path. It was the size and shape of a squished cantaloupe. He trod gingerly forward so's to be in a position to intercept the raccoon, aware that Lara72 was treading with him. Without looking at her, he said, "How do we decide?"

"I'm not sure," she said. "Maybe we don't."

Wayne nodded knowingly. "Wait, what do you mean?"

"Well, maybe *we* don't decide. Maybe it's all decided for us."

"I see." The raccoon was coming around again, thrashing through the bushes towards them. If something other than Wayne was going to make this decision, it'd better make it soon. The raccoon emerged, and Wayne raised his rock. Before he could even think about bringing it down, though, the creature had scooted past them and back into the woods. Even on two legs it was wicked fast.

"Holy shit," said Lara72, quite sublimely.

Next time he'd be ready. Rock aloft, Wayne called to mind what his Little League coach had taught him, or tried to. You couldn't wait for a good pitch and then swing, you had to start swinging and stop if it was a bad pitch. You had to be in motion already.

The rock was on its way down as the raccoon broke through the underbrush again. One of Wayne's problems as a Little Leaguer had been that he tended to close his eyes at the start of his swing, and this is what he did now. His follow-through was good, though – the rock hit the ground with a solid thud. The ground, and a little bit of his foot.

"Oh my fucking *God!*" he shouted. He wanted to collapse, but willed himself to stay upright.

"Yes!" shouted Lara72. She had her hands clasped together, and was gazing rapturously down the path after the raccoon. It was at a full gallop, all four legs going hard. It didn't slow as it crested and disappeared over the next hill.

"Huh," said Wayne, fighting the urge to sob.

Lara72 sighed. "See? Everything happens just the way it's meant to."

Wayne made do with bending over in agony – perhaps it would look like some sort of ecstatic fit. Walking wouldn't be easy in the near future – it seemed likely he'd never walk right again – but Lara72 was oblivious to his blunder, and he aimed to keep it that way for as long as possible.

"Wayne?" she said.

"Yes, exactly," he said, shoving himself upright. Sure, there were silly, smug ideas in this world – *meant* to happen? and you'd know that how? – but what if you just went along with them? What if you pretended to believe? What if you actually did believe? Might you end up with a woman as fine as this one?

Wayne took a deep breath – a brief numbness in his foot was giving way, once again, to excruciating pain. "Everything," he said, "is perfect."

Elephant

It's weird how even if you have no choice about something, you still want to choose. Like for instance it's not up to me if I get born as a girl or a boy next time, but I'm still going to hope for one or the other. But which?

Last time I was a girl and it didn't last long, not nearly long enough. My mother wouldn't nurse me, hardly even peeped at me before she handed me over to the woman next door. The oleander flower is pretty, but its juice tastes like … like what? I can't even say because it's the only thing I ever had in my mouth, except for the bit of water the woman used to wash it down. Like hard with sharp in it. Like cold with loud in it. Like a mother's milk must be, but the exact opposite of that. My heart bumped inside of me, fast and then slow, slow. Strange to have it inside when all those months it had been outside, my mother's heart, thwushhh, thwushhh, everywhere always.

I can't blame my mother, because how can you blame someone until you're that person in that situation? I like to think I'd let my daughter live, but how do I know? Maybe I'd sew a little outfit for her, and put flowers in her hair. Maybe I'd drown her in a bucket, like the woman next door did with me when the oleander took too long. If I'm born a girl again maybe I'll grow up to be a woman and have a daughter, and I'll find out.

I don't blame my mother, but I worry about her. How many million lives of being good will it take her to undo this? Unless it turns out to be okay to throw out baby girls, but then I don't even know what to say about that.

What I really want is never to be born again, but of course that's what everyone wants. Wanting it isn't enough, in fact wanting it shows you need to keep on being born so you can learn not to want it. Being alive gets you nowhere, but you have to live long enough to figure that out. Then you can let yourself seep away into everything and stay there forever.

A girl, I think. Yes, I'd like to be a girl again but grow up, and that could happen. So many girls aren't allowed to live that there aren't even enough of them anymore. Before long women will be rare, and rare things are valuable things, so women will be wanted for wives and prostitutes and slaves and so on. A slave would be good, in fact a slave would be best because to see that pain is an illusion you have to be in pain. I'd like to be born a girl and grow up to be a slave and suffer and find liberation and never come back.

Or a boy, but I can't remember what that's like, assuming I've been a boy before, which I suppose I must have been.

Your true self can't be one or the other, can it? But imagine, you're a boy and you grow up as though it's the right thing to do. How do you hate yourself, I wonder? How do you learn?

No, I'm hoping girl. Girl, girl, girl, but I bet I'll be an elephant or something, for having cried when my mother gave me to the woman next door. I'll be an elephant, and I'll live in some other place where elephants are kept in cages and stared at as though they're strange, and no one can make any sense of the sounds that come out of them.

First Kiss

To get to the cemetery you had to drive along our street, under the dark archway of chestnuts and maples. It must have been enchanting for the mourners, or depressing, or something. And then the thonk of plums as we pelted the procession.

Our theory was that people would be too grief-stricken to come after us, or too worried about their good clothes. This is when we were twelve or so, too old for such idiocy, but anyway. We'd load an apple basket with plums fallen from the Barfoots' tree, and we'd duck down behind the foundation wall in the abandoned lot next to Shithead's house a few blocks down from mine. There'd be Shithead, and Dunk, and Kev maybe, and me. Somebody would yell "Fire!" and we'd fire. The plums were soft and slippery, half-rotten, so you couldn't really pitch them, more like catapult them, cupping them in your palm. Most of them would miss, but not all of them.

I don't know how many funerals we bombed that year, it seemed like a lot but it was probably only a half dozen or so. Mostly the vehicles would just keep going, crawling along like a battalion of tanks in a movie. The hearse (you got double points if you hit that, though we never actually kept score), then a limo or two, and then a bunch of just normal cars, a line of variable length depending on how much the person had been loved, I suppose, or by how many people.

But this one time a limo stopped, the limo right behind the hearse. The hearse kept going – maybe he didn't check his mirror, or maybe he didn't feel right hitting the brakes with a dead body in back. But the limo stopped, and the whole procession behind it. Out of the limo crawled this guy. Like my father, that sort of age, but smaller and more angular, and dressed head to foot in black. He looked over our way – we'd neglected to duck back down, too surprised I guess. And he came charging.

We had a plan, which was to split up. That was our whole plan. I don't know where the others went but I took off for home, down the back lane. When it occurred to me how stupid that was I cut through a couple of yards over towards the school. The mourner had singled me out – I was the stoutest and slowest of our miscreant little gang – and he was coming hard, I could hear him. At one point the nerve just went out of me. The mourner found me sitting in a patch of leafy greens in somebody's garden, crying like a five-year-old.

And what he did was he comforted me. He assured me that he too had been young once, young and senseless. He was still huffing from the run, and he patted my arm and told me to go ahead and cry, that there was no shortage of things to cry about in this world. He asked me if I minded if he had a little cry too, and he had one, a few dry-eyed sobs which turned into a laugh. "Is that really the way I *weep?*" he said, and he wept some more, and laughed some more. He had a beard, which he gripped as though to keep his face from slipping off.

By this time my fear had deepened to the kind you don't cry about. I sat still while he told me about somebody named Neil, a friend from his childhood. It may have been Neil's body in the hearse, but I've never been sure of that. What I do know is that Neil had a major overbite as a boy, and that he was crazy about birds. He could identify a bird from a silhouette in flight, or from a snippet of song. Warbler, thrush, you name it.

After a while the mourner came to himself, remembering about his funeral, I suppose. "Yep, that Neil," he said, shaking his head. Then he gave me another pat, stood up and trotted away.

It was dinner time but I took the long route home, past the park. There was a girl named Yasmin, an almost-cute girl from my grade, just saying goodbye to some friends at the baseball diamond. "Wanna walk?" she said, and she came up beside me. We only half knew each other and hadn't much to talk about. Mostly she kept staring at me, and finally she said, "Have you been crying?"

I wiped my face and said that somebody had died.

"Oh," she said. "I'm sorry about that. Who died?"

I said, "I don't know."

Yasmin laughed. I remember her laugh sounded like some people's bawling. I stepped in front of her and turned and kissed her on the mouth, which I'd never done to anybody before. Yasmin kissed me back, or at least she didn't pull away. She and her friends must have had cigarettes, because she tasted like my mother's breath after she'd been out on the porch by herself. I put my hand on her cheek, Yasmin's cheek, a hand still sticky and sweet with overripe plum.

My wife, Gina, doesn't buy it. She refuses to believe that what happened that day is at the root of what she calls my "problem." Why call it a "problem" in the first place, if it isn't actually a problem? That's what I keep asking her. And she keeps laughing, which I love (Gina laughs like a cat after a bird it can't quite reach). All that matters is that I want her, and that I'll never stop. I'll never stop.

Word of Mouth

Stan's first career was inspired by the swoop of a heron past the window of the family cottage when he was a kid. Fish were floating to the surface of Long Lake that year, and talk was that soon birds and other predators too would be succumbing to the chemicals that had been allowed to seep into a feeder stream. Stan was already disturbed by this thought, and by the fact that he and his brother had been barred from the water, but it was the thrill of the heron's heavy flight that truly got to him, the notion that something so alive could soon be dead, and dead because of people. Ten years later he emerged from school with a degree in marine biology. Thirty years after that he cleared out his desk at Rant Cow Hive.

Fired, laid off, whatever – the agency (actually Envirowatch, but Stan and his colleagues diverted themselves creating various anagrams) was being eviscerated, middle-aged, mid-rank characters such as himself being set unceremoniously free. A trauma, not because Stan loved the job (he resented it, the long slow fiasco it made of his life), but because he'd just ended his marriage, and vacated his house, and was running short on things of which to be dispossessed.

Stan's second career was inspired by Mr. Neziri, the man across the hall from his mother at the hospital, where Stan spent more and more time in the aftermath of his sacking. Mr. Neziri and Stan's mother were both doomed, but they were going about their deaths in radically different ways. Stan's mother, for instance, was deaf and almost mute. Save the odd noisy non sequitur ("Won't you stay for dinner?!?" when she was being fed through a nose tube), she held her peace about her predicament. Mr. Neziri, on the other hand. What was that sound he made? A sob, a moan? A sob-moan, a yowl-howl, a wail-whimper. It was nothing, there was no word. Actually, there was what sounded like a word once, out in the middle of one interminable jag, in a language unknown to Stan. And then back to the meaningless caterwaul once more.

Meaningless, that was the key. To mark death you had to make a sound that transmitted no meaning at all, that was in fact a constant obliteration of meaning. Mr. Neziri was mourning himself, articulating his oblivion before it descended upon him. But what of those, such as Stan's own mum, who hadn't the sagacity or the fortitude for this task? Who would cry out for them? Didn't there used to be professional mourners? Why shouldn't there be once more?

Stan's old boss Bernie (who'd also been axed) had been sending Stan links to articles called things like "Second Time Around" and "Age as an Asset" and "Repurposing the Middle-Aged Man." What you didn't have any more was energy. What made up for that was wisdom, worldliness. Your first career had been about duty. Your new one would be about love. You were done with obligation, time to follow your bliss.

Love? Bliss? Well, demand, at least there'd be lots of that. Stan was one of about a billion people soon to be robbed of somebody. His fellow boomers for a start, with all their ailing parents and friends.

He began his rehearsals at "home," the not-quite-wretched bachelor suite out of which he kept on not moving. He'd knock back a half-mickey of vodka (a poor man's peyote, is how he thought of it, opening him to shamanic energies), bring the lights down to a funereal gloom and get started.

The idea was to have no idea. Stan's sound needed to be free of all influence and intent, each act of mourning incomprehensible in its own unique way. He'd made the mistake of starting with online research, and now needed to erase the memory of other wailers (the Yaminawa of Peru, the Nar-wij-jerook of Australia), along, of course, with the memory of every other human utterance he'd ever witnessed. To be meaningless, a cry needed to be innocent of all allusion and all shape. Free jazz but freer, no key, no time signature, no consistency of tone, tempo, timbre. Stan had a decent voice (he'd rated a solo on "Softly and Tenderly" with the boys' choir back at St. Joe's), which was both a blessing and a curse. What he was singing now was scat but more so, a series of sounds denuded of history and prospects, a pure racket. At every moment he needed to say nothing.

There was a dry spell, sure. Stan ran a few ads ("When it's for eternity, you want the best!"), but he knew it was personal contact that usually got you your start. And so it was. A first nibble came from his brother, who wrote to say that he'd be staying on with his firm in Fukuoka for another year because of a death one rung up the ladder. Stan replied with an update on his new career, hinting that he'd be open to a contract abroad, to which his brother came back with, "You need help, man. Seriously, I love you, but you need help." Promising. Any real insight was bound to be met at first with dismay, no? How had people responded when they first learned the fate of the natural world?

And then the breakthrough. When the police showed up a third time in response to complaints from neighbors (whose wall-pounding served as accompaniment many nights), Stan got chatting with one constable while the other wrote up his warning. An almost frighteningly empathetic individual, this guy turned out to have a sick sister who was busy planning her own gala funeral. "A professional mourner," he mused. "Hey, she might just go for that!"

The audition took place in the sister's hospital room. On another ward, in another part of the city, Stan's mother and Mr. Neziri were still at it. Stan had two months of daily practice under his belt by this time, and was beginning to feel some confidence. Indeed, the audition went well. One little phrase from "All Along the Watchtower" snuck in, but his bellowing was otherwise bereft of sense, of any discernible pattern or meaning. The siblings were perfectly devastated, as were the mourners at the sister's funeral a month or so later.

From there, things just sort of took off.

Red Giant

Other than turtles – I must have had ten of them, one after another, all failing to thrive despite the plastic palm tree under which they lounged in their little plastic bowl – Stranger was the first pet I ever lost. He'd come to us old, a West Highland terrier with a bit of Chihuahua in him. "Howdy, stranger," Dad said to him when he crept into our yard one day, and when he stayed the name stuck. He had bad hips, an unfortunate skin condition, and a dyspeptic temper. Dad warned us not to get attached to him, me and my brothers, or rather he warned us we would get attached, so we'd get hurt. Dad was an almost pathologically realistic man. His idea was to keep things in perspective, the bigger the perspective the better.

Which is why he got us into astronomy. He had a telescope through which he invited us to peer on clear weekend nights. It wasn't a particularly powerful one: you were lucky to discern a couple of Jupiter's many moons, a fine halo around

Saturn where you knew its rings must be. The tininess of these magnified objects did convey a sense of scale, and Dad added to this impression with mythic-sounding tales about heavenly bodies. He told us, for instance, that almost everything in the universe was invisible. "Dark matter," he called it, explaining that astronomers knew of its existence only because of the gravity it exerted on visible objects. "Everything you see," he said to us, "is dictated by things you don't."

When Stranger died, I took it particularly hard, perhaps because I was the youngest of us three boys. I was eight. I've looked it up, and that happens to be the age at which a child finally gets the hang of death's trickiest aspect, its universality. *Everything* dies? Dad reinforced this point, the day we buried Stranger (in the yard where he'd first appeared, next to the big spiky bush), by describing to me the death of the sun.

"What can help at a time like this," he said – we were tamping down the sod over Stranger's corpse – "is to broaden your view. Take in the bigger picture. For instance ..." Here he gestured at a smear of tangerine just fading from the western sky. "The sun. It's a long way off, right?"

"Ninety three million miles." I was eager to demonstrate that I'd been listening, that his efforts to enlighten me had not been entirely misplaced.

"Correct." He gave my shoulder a gentle punch. "But it won't always be so distant. As it runs out of fuel, the sun will heat up and expand. Eventually it will be so big we'll be inside it."

"Inside the sun," I said. It sometimes helped to repeat Dad's outlandish truths out loud.

He nodded. "Inside the sun. A red giant, you call it, a star that expands at the end of its life." He allowed an imaginary sphere to inflate between his hands, then squeezed it down to almost nothing. "At the very finish it collapses and cools to become what's called a white dwarf. The sun will end up about the size of good old earth here." He patted the ground with the ball of his foot.

"What about ...?"

"About ...? Oh, us? People? No, this isn't for billions of years yet. The sun's still got half its life to go. We won't be ... that won't be a problem."

I can't say this comforted me, exactly, this vision of a post-human world burned back to its original nothingness, but it did help. My grief was intact, but it no longer quite consumed me. Or perhaps it's just that I was smaller, so my grief was smaller too.

I used this technique to deal with other trials as a kid, and I use it today. I find I have more frequent recourse to it as time goes on. Like the sun, I'm middle-aged now, my fuel beginning perceptibly to dwindle. A sort of low-grade grief is with me a great deal of the time, even though I'd describe myself as happy. This is what Dad was preparing me for, I think – for this, and for the losses yet to come. I still have him, and my mother, and my brothers, and my wife, and so on. There's a great deal for which to brace oneself.

I sometimes wonder if even the scale of the solar system will do. In the dentist's chair yesterday afternoon, for the third session of a botched root canal, I tried going bigger. I told Dad about my new innovation on the phone last night, my lips burning as sensation returned to them. "I've been brushing up," I said. "Remember the heat death of the universe?"

"Heat death," said Dad. "Heat. Death. Remind me?"

It's hard to tell, these days, if he's just humouring me again, giving me the pleasure of putting something into words, or if he's actually forgotten. "Entropy," I said. "When you expend energy there's always a little of it lost, right? Made useless? So things run down."

"They do."

"So the theory is, that applies to the whole universe. It's like a cup of tea cooling in the kitchen. Eventually the tea and the kitchen come to the same temperature, so nothing more can happen. That's the end."

"Of everything."

"Of everything."

There was a pause. There's often a pause when Dad and I chat these days, an open sort of silence, each of us leaving space.

Ghost

Veronica Swit, our restive Ronnie, who for two decades penned obituaries for this very page, salvaging individuality time and again from the annihilating mire of oblivion, has died of asphyxiation at age fifty-three. "The idiosyncratic self," she once wrote (in her obit for novelist David Foster Wallace), "comes into being at the moment of its first secret, its first lie, and has no choice but to keep existing until it no longer does." Yet elsewhere she spoke of death as the lie. "Nina Simone is still singing," she said. "If you can't hear her right here, right now, well then that's just sad." Ronnie, too, still sings, still answers to our longing.

Ronnie lost neither of her parents when she was young (in Cut Knife, by the North Saskatchewan River), nor did she lose siblings or close friends. To what, then, can we trace the intensity of her desire to join the "dead beat" fresh out of journalism school (Ryerson, 1988)? Raised on a fundamentalist image of hell, and bedeviled by it throughout her life, she certainly sought a more benign notion of eternity. Beyond that, she had a deep, appalled fascination with narrative, with the shapeliness of a "completed life" (a term she wryly lifted from the assisted dying debate). "Death satisfies every desire," is how Ronnie opened her Ingmar Bergman obit. "It resolves every tension, delivers to every story its denouement."

So, stories. There was the time she showed up at the office Halloween party as the blue Twitter bird, and spoke only in gnomic little non sequiturs all night long. (In her obit for Instagram influencer Sinead McNamara, Ronnie lauded social media as "an invaluable foretaste of death, constantly reminding us where we aren't, and who we aren't with.") There was the time she spent her summer vacation getting herself teargassed and water cannoned alongside the Standing Rock Sioux. There was the time she brought her rescue pit bull, Baudelaire, to work in a beret and cravat, and snarled at anybody (including yours truly) who couldn't summon the nerve to cuddle him.

Some of Ronnie's tales, it must be revealed, were fiction. She was named after Veronica Lake, the femme fatale with the peek-a-boo blonde locks. (Her namesake was actually the New Testament Veronica who wiped the blood from Christ's face at the 6th Station of the Cross.) Her first published piece, in the *Paris Review*, was a love story set in an afterlife in which the dead exist as sounds with no substance, no history, no gender. ("Litter Literally Kills" was the title of her first piece, appearing in the *North Battleford News-Optimist*.) What's not fictional is Ronnie's infatuation with irony, which she touted as the ultimate tool of the sceptic, the wonderer. In a sense her whole project was ironic, her words about the dead subjecting life to tireless inquisition. What she said was always so much less than what she meant.

Ronnie was astonishingly productive, her output suggestive of some subterranean source of heat, some hidden font or friction. It helped that she was awake so much of the time. As she summed it up in a (nicely flawed) syllogism scrawled on a sticky by her bed,

> All ghosts are insomniacs.
>
> I am an insomniac.
>
> I am a ghost.

Ghostlike she could be, even ghoulish. She haunted funerals and wakes, as inconspicuous as a second cousin. (As the only other woman working the obits, I ventured to describe her once as "Audrey Hepburn cast in a plain part.") The bereaved are only briefly truthful about the beloved, and soon fall back on bromides – Ronnie knew she had to be quick to learn anything of interest about the dead. (I flatter myself that she'd have appreciated this wordplay, though if she'd said so it would have been under her breath.) Survivors were often startled by her raw reporting. Where another obit might say "jolly raconteur" she'd go with "boozing blowhard." With the living too she could be caustic – at least one ex-husband was characterized as a "dull obit just waiting to happen."

It's been made much of that Ronnie was fascinated with suicide. Her own death, however, was almost certainly accidental – or at least, like that of Ophelia (another fervent, fractured soul), it deserves to be left a mystery. Did her flight from the last of her three marriages loosen Ronnie's grip on life? Did her dalliance with psychedelics (originally undertaken as research for her Steve Jobs piece) too dramatically decentre her already harrowed sense of self? We have no way of knowing. There's every reason to believe she'd be pleased about this.

All of us here at the paper, including those of us who will try and fail to fill her shoes, are saddened by her passing.

Correction: When it originally ran in our print edition, this piece mistakenly referred to Veronica Swit's dog, Baudelaire, as Rimbaud. In addition, the piece made reference to an "enduring if undeclared love," for which there is no substantiation. Our apologies to her family.

Squeeze

What she needs is a baby. There's an antidote to everything, someone once said, or should have, and the antidote to time with a person who's about to die is time with a person who's just been born. The catch is that Gretta's own kids, all three of them grown and stably partnered, are childless. She's been scrupulous about not nagging them, refraining from any little remark that might inspire in them guilt or remorse for their disinclination to procreate. She's beginning to see how wrong-headed this approach has been. Time to crank up the pressure. Gretta arises and retires each day feeling inadequate. Why shouldn't they?

For now, at any rate, there's no grandchild to whom she can rush after another brutal night with her elderly and un-well and almost supernaturally ungrateful mother-in-law. Gretta's best bet is her friend Lucy's daughter's new son. Gretta's only seen pictures of him – a chinless, darkly-tufted little bloke – which gives her an excuse to intrude and meet him in person. It's Monday, Lucy's day to cover for her daughter. Worth dropping by this morning just on the off chance.

But there's no answer at Lucy's door. Gretta rings, then knocks, then makes her way through the gate at the side of the house and around back, not because she expects to discover Lucy and the little boy there but because she has no plan B, no alternate scheme for distracting or consoling herself. What she ought to do is head home and have yet another go at the paperwork for her mother-in-law's home support application, or her mother-in-law's medical benefits application, or her mother-in-law's disability tax credit application, stopping en route to drop off her mother-in-law's urine sample and pick up more pull-ups and more bleach and more Boost or Ensure, assuming she remembered to put the coupon for one or the other in her purse, but she believes the prospect of these tasks will cause her to drive into a tree, specifically the big leafless chestnut at Royal and 8th. She's pictured it already, more than once. Midway through the left turn onto 8th she fakes an aneurysm. She slumps over, stomps on the accelerator, plows through the flower bed into the massive trunk. So sad, but we don't believe she suffered.

"Lucy's not home."

"Pardon? Hello?" Gretta scans for the source of the voice.

"I saw her leave a while ago."

"Ah."

On the back porch next door there's a young woman, about the age of Gretta's eldest. She holds a wriggly infant in her arms. As Gretta draws closer, rearing up to see over the hedge, she notes that while the woman is red of hair and pale of skin, the infant is Asian. Chinese, probably. So many abandoned baby girls. Such a kindness to take them in.

"I'm Lucy's friend," says Gretta. "What a lovely child. I think it's wonderful."

"Wonderful?" says the woman.

"What you've done. What people like you do."

"People like me?" These words could communicate offense, but they don't. Curious, is what the young woman seems to be.

"I just mean reaching out like that," says Gretta. "I have a friend who adopted a baby with fetal alcohol syndrome. Such a burden. Not a burden, but ..." She rubs at her forehead. This headache is going nowhere. "How old is she?"

"He's fifteen months."

A young man steps out onto the back porch beside the woman. Asian. Korean? The father. Wrong story.

Gretta says, "Could I hold your son?"

The two young parents turn to look at one another. In concert, they look down at the child. What's their most basic inclination as parents? To share or to shelter? It's perhaps too early for them to be certain.

"Just for a minute?" says Gretta. "Just for a second?" She strives in vain to keep the desperation from her voice.

The man murmurs something to his wife in what Gretta assumes to be Korean. The woman nods. She appears to be pregnant again, her belly warping the blue stripes of her white sweater, or the white stripes of her blue sweater, as gravity is said to warp the geometries of space-time. Gretta will be doing everything possible, everything short of assault, to get a hand on that bulge. The stir, the tremor of new life – she's woozy with wanting it.

The man steps off the deck and comes towards her. When he reaches the hedge he grabs and pulls back an armful of it so Gretta can slip through. Gretta stoops and presses her way into the gap, but it's tight. It's too tight – Gretta has the panicky feeling she won't make it through, that the pain behind her eyes will turn black and obliterate her. She squirms forward, but is she getting anywhere? She needs help, a shove from behind, and now she seems to be getting one. It's almost as though she's being born, or rather, it's exactly as though she's being born. She's being born. There's a brutal light, and she's being pushed towards it, squeezed out of a dense darkness like a pit being squeezed from a plum.

Words fall short here. Early experience, the experience of a newborn, turns out to be almost entirely immune to the incursions of language. Gretta continues to know, in some sense, that she used to be Gretta, but this knowing gets fuzzy over time, the way a dream will do as the day goes by. Ji-hwan is her new name, or rather his. Ji-hwan's older brother repeats this name to him tirelessly. By the time Ji-hwan can say it – he'll be eighteen months old, and he'll pronounce it "chew on" – he'll no longer be anybody else. He'll be himself, and he'll continue to be only that until he too reaches the limit of his ability to bear it.

Open

Fear of death comes sixth on the list, but it's really the only fear so it's all of them. Fear of flying, for instance, which is number one. Why would anybody be afraid to fly if they didn't think they might crash? Or number two, public speaking. Go back to when we were a tribe someplace and those staring eyes are the eyes of lions or wolves, a bunch of something hungry for you. And heights, and the dark, those are obvious. And intimacy, the fear of which is that you'll disappear.

So I figured if I wasn't afraid to die I wouldn't be afraid of anything. To get free of Carl all I had to do was overcome that one fear. Which is where You came in.

What's odd and kind of beautiful is that Carl introduced me to You in the first place. His dad believed, and even though Carl didn't he kept the Book around, an awful gold thing from a motel. *We are afflicted in every way,* I read, sitting on the toilet with the shower steaming up my glasses, *but not crushed.* And then, *This mortal nature must put on immortality.* The way to do this is through faith, I found out, which is helplessness. I can do nothing so I'm saved. I'm mortal so I'm immortal. I carry Your death around in me so I'm resurrected with You every moment of every day forever. None of this is possible so it's true.

It was Carl who taught me how to have faith, in a funny way. Carl is what's called a spiritual entrepreneur, which means he makes money by believing he's going to make money. The thing is, he's not very good at it. He doesn't make money, which is because he doesn't believe in himself, which is because I don't believe in him, which is why he sometimes hits me with his stapler or his three-hole punch. Or he did, until last night when You helped me leave.

Between Luke and John in Carl's dad's copy there's a picture of You on the cross. The soldiers have come back to break Your legs to help You die, but You're dead already. To make sure, they stick You with a lance and out pours blood and water, which is the human and divine of You. What gets me every time is that gash in Your side, like a mouth, which in a way it is since it talks to me. I peer into it, into Your body, the same way I peer into my own body when Carl opens it up, like that time he split my forehead to a white that was my skull. There's only inside and outside, there's nothing to fret about.

Carl caught up to me in the lobby when I stepped out of the elevator. In my bag I had the Book and only a few other things, including the red panties I wore our very first time.

"I'll die," he said.

I said, "Maybe." Which now that I think about it, do we actually die even when we die?

"I'll kill you," he said.

I said, "Maybe. Here I go."

And I went. I caught a bus to Cindy's from work, who's taken me in until I can find my own place. We sat up and drank tea last night as though we were just two girls, which is what we were. Her biggest fear is abandonment, number twenty, though shouldn't it be higher? Poor Carl. I hope You can help him too. Please help him.

Number eleven is fear of flowers, which is strange, but I guess even flowers can kill people, or at least people can believe it. People can believe anything. Number nineteen is fear of You, which is foolish since You're why we don't have to fear anything at all. Though of course it's also true that You can kill us whenever You want to, and You will. No matter what kills me, it will be You.

The Physical Part

There was a lot of weird shit about Shauna. Mostly good weird, though you couldn't always tell at first. Right by her bed, where most people would keep a book or maybe a bottle of lube, she kept a picture of her Great-Great-Aunt Lucy. In the photo, which was actually a daguerreotype, an antique silvery sort of image, Lucy was an infant. She had a pudgy face and blank teddy-bear eyes glinting straight out at you. She was in a fabric-lined box you gradually recognized as a coffin.

"Holy bloody wow," I said the first time I saw it. We'd just made love, sort of, and Shauna was in the bathroom loudly peeing.

"No, it's okay," she called out. "Don't feel bad. The physical part —"

"I'm saying the picture. Is he …?"

Shauna wandered back in, tying up a pair of white karate pants. She was the most beautiful woman I'd ever seen naked, which was odd because she looked like a boy. And okay, maybe that's what threw me off for a bit. Is there such a thing as a beautiful person, as opposed to a beautiful woman or a beautiful man? That would be Shauna.

"Picture?" she said. "Oh, Lucy. My mother's father's mother's sister."

"Your mother's ..."

"Father's mother's sister."

"And she's dead there? She died little?"

"Yup." Shauna started to pull on a T-shirt, but changed her mind. She knelt by the futon, her breasts softening ever-so-slightly the striated structure of her chest. "Wanna go again? We can do better."

"But what's ... why?" I forced my gaze back to Lucy. The photo was small, and cut into an oval, as though somebody had once worn it in a locket. Shauna had taped it to the bedside lamp.

"They used to do that, take a picture once a person passed. See the hand behind her head?"

I squinted. "Like a halo, almost."

"Mhm, yeah. So that would be her mother's hand, my mother's great-grandmother's." Shauna shook out her hair, deep purple at the tips but growing in blonde. "She turned religious after that, Lucy's mum. Wandered around muttering *Santa Maria madre de Dios* all the time, we're Spanish on my mum's side. You couldn't get her to say anything else. Will you have the pork or the beef, ma'am? *Madre de Dios.*"

"Creepy. The picture, I mean."

"Not really."

"You don't —"

Shauna leaned forward and slipped a nipple between my lips.

Our second time was better.

Our third was better again.

"Right beside your *bed*, though?" I had my head on Shauna's belly, my cheek against her sweat-slick skin. Her stomach gurgled sweetly in my ear. I had no plans to go anywhere, ever.

"People used to have pictures like that around," she said. "They knew how to look at them."

It wasn't that day but maybe a week later that she told me about *samvega*, a Pali word that means the shock you feel when you realize life is pointless, but then try to come up with a point.

"It's the consternation," Shauna said, "but also the urgency. Death's one of the only things that can hit you hard enough, supposably." She'd do that with her words, say them like a little kid, especially when she caught herself in the middle of some big idea. Ambliance. Excape.

"I guess," I said. We were in bed again. We were in bed most of the time in those early days, between shifts at YUMMY!, where we often manned opposite ends of the Hobart Sensotronic. She could load dirty dishes faster than I could unload clean ones, which drove me mad. Almost everything about her drove me mad.

"You suddenly realize this is all you have," said Shauna. She patted the rumpled bedspread, which I took to be representative of the human condition in all its radical contingency.

"You'd better get on with it."

"It?"

Her stomach whistled like a whale.

"What if the it is us?" I said. "What if it's us?"

"Huh," she said.

It wasn't for another month or so that she told me she was pregnant. "Six weeks," she said, and let that sink in. We'd been together five.

"Ah," I said. I was shocked, but not deeply enough. It wasn't until the baby was born that I felt it all the way down. Little Lucy (it was to be that or Lionel, after my dad), covered in goo from the inside of Shauna's body. Lucy had been nothing, and now she was something, and someday she'd be nothing again. Shock, and this sudden sense that maybe in some weird way stuff actually mattered.

The other thing with Shauna was that she lied a lot. She still does. There was no Aunt Lucy – Shauna had snipped the photo from a liberry book and made up a story to go with it. Also, she wasn't pregnant when we met, that was to give me an excuse to bail if I wasn't all in. We figure she got pregnant that very first day we made love.

"Lucy," Shauna said, after she'd confessed to her ruse. I was squatting there by the birth bed, this bizarre sweet beautiful little person in my arms. "Juicy Lucy Goosey. She's yours."

Another lie, of course, since nobody is anybody's. Like a lot of Shauna's lies, it was a good one, helpfully half true. How long will I feel the need to believe it?

Peacemaker

Roberto says yes, Kunchen says no. Are we moving faster now? Have the fuddles finally got things sorted out, adjusted to the sudden rush? If they have, is that a good thing, should we want to get where we're going? Roberto says yes, Kunchen says no.

Sometimes I think they disagree just for the heck of it. All of us are desperate for ways to pass the time, if time is what we're passing. From behind me Roberto says, "The women are ahead of us." From ahead of me Kunchen says, "The women are behind us." Neither of them knows, none of us knows. All we know is that the women aren't here, that all three of these lines are men's lines. At first we were able to switch from one to another, strive to get ourselves into the fastest one – or the slowest, depending on what we'd decided to believe about our destination – but then we reached the dividers and had to choose.

By fuddles we don't know what we mean. Who or what is in charge here? We haven't the faintest.

The dividers are transparent, and go all the way up. I once had a clear plastic thing where you dropped a coin in the top and it found its way to the correct cylinder: penny, nickel, dime, quarter. Perhaps my memories will keep coming back to me in this way.

We've inched forward again.

"Things are speeding up," says Roberto.

"Things are slowing down," says Kunchen.

"Things are staying the same," says Otto. Otto is me.

Theories get passed up and down the line. The fuddles planned for certain eventualities, but not for all of them. They expected us to arrive faster as things got worse where we came from, but they forgot what might happen all at once. How could they forget such a thing? How could we forget it? Here's how I think of the situation: there are certain some-things inside you which could destroy you but for some reason don't, so why should you stew about them? And then they do.

Roberto says one-third, Kunchen says two-thirds. "Half?" I say. There will be many more – there will be everybody before long – so in a way we were lucky to arrive with the first big group. If lucky is what that makes us.

Mostly we talk about the women. We don't have pictures of them – we don't have anything – so we seek to describe them for one another. This is a challenge, because even in our minds they've lost their features, and their names too, as we've lost ours. We've made up names for them, just as we've made up names for ourselves. My wife is Francoise now, just as I'm Otto. I say wife, but could she be my daughter? My sister? My mother? Could she be me?

Except coconuts, we do have coconuts. Why coconuts? It's as though the point of all these questions is to have no answers. Roberto says the best part of the coconut is the foul but refreshing water, Kunchen says it's the sweet flesh. "They're both superb," I say. In this as in all things I am the peacemaker, though to be honest I lean towards the sweet flesh.

We each remember one thing. Roberto remembers the light, Kunchen remembers the sound – an inconceivable roar, he says, though we do conceive it – and I remember the heat. Who remembers the wind? There may have been a moment at which parts of me were being blown off, or I may be making that up. There's nothing to do here but make things up. Who started it? Who took sides with whom?

We've inched forward again.

"Hope," says Roberto.

"Fear," says Kunchen.

"Hope and fear," I say. "Hope and fear."

Rat Dead Wall Disease

The smell originated in the bathroom and advanced outwards through the little basement suite. Kitchen, living room, bedroom. The odious intensity of it gradually declined with increasing distance from its source. Like waves of Wi-Fi, Trev signed to Hannah, and she nodded. At night in bed they could light a stick of incense and almost forget.

The scent was presumably emanating upwards too, but they couldn't confirm this since their landlord, Mr. Dufort, who lived alone above them, was abroad visiting family. Hannah tried emailing him, but no luck. Trev called a plumber, and they had him complete his inspection before confessing that they couldn't pay. It wasn't clear why he was so furious, since he hadn't done anything, simply confirmed that there was nothing he could do. Sampling the air like a dog trained to sniff out heroin or cancer he announced, "Nope. That's not sewer. Something dead in the wall, be my guess.

Just let it dry out." He gave the lining of the shower stall an exploratory rap. "Got rodents, I'm guessing?" But they didn't, so far as they knew. This was the first place they'd shared in their four years together that seemed to be vermin free, save the inevitable ants and silverfish. Trev signed the news to Hannah, who said, "Rats here in paradise?" in that voice she'd never heard.

Truth be told, Trev had detected a scratching in the structure of the house one night the previous week, but he hadn't yet shared this news with Hannah. That day had been a dismal one, his first and last day of work in many months. As a younger man – he was past thirty now – Trev had toyed briefly with the idea of acting school. This history had emboldened him to apply, one recent caffeine-crazed afternoon, for the position of Standardized Patient Actor. At the interview he'd lied successfully about his lack of relevant training or experience, which seemed to establish that he didn't need any. What most preoccupied the interviewer was Trev's memory, since it would be his job to accurately report and mimic, for a series of medical students, various medical conditions. Trev was able to demonstrate the ghastly thoroughness of his recall by rhyming off, in alphabetical order, the titles of the pamphlets in the waiting room. *Alcohol and Substance Abuse. Anxiety and Panic Attacks. Depression Dos and Don'ts.* At this last Trev winced and emitted a low groan, which the interviewer seemed to take as a good sign, a sign that Trev was empathetic but exempt from these troubles. He offered Trev his hand for a congratulatory shake.

After three half-days of instruction at the university, Trev was assigned his first role. "Arthur" was a young man who suffered from a sinus infection he believed to be a brain tumour of the kind that had killed his father. Trev nailed the part. He drew on his grief for his own dad, with whom he'd barely spoken since their falling out over Hannah, and more generally over what his father perceived to be the perverse aimlessness of Trev's life. The first medical student to try her diagnostic skills on Arthur, a chipper young woman named Biyu, struck Trev as oddly unmoved by Arthur's fraught condition. Improvising, Trev wove in details from his own life. The chest pains, the night terrors. Such was his immersion in the role that he began to sob, and could not be stopped. Biyu stroked his arm, hissed into an intercom. Trev was thanked and sent home.

He almost fell asleep that night – he rarely did until daylight – but startled at what he imagined to be a scrabbling sound, nails on wood. Wide awake, he could no longer distinguish it. The gentle huff of Hannah's breath, the irritable click and buzz of the refrigerator, the drone of night traffic, nothing else. Had the scrabbling sound entered him from the apartment? Or was it the other way around, had it spilled out into the apartment from within? Looking back, Trev found himself seriously entertaining this notion. Parts of him had escaped his body, to die and rot in the walls. It felt possible.

The plumber having angrily departed, Trev and Hannah spent the rest of the afternoon on her phone looking up "rat dead wall disease" and various permutations thereof. After a leftover take-out Thai dinner they binged on closed-captioned reruns of *Full House*, a saccharine sitcom which reminded neither of them of their youth. Hannah, currently on the morning shift at the Homemade Buns factory, turned in early.

Trev lay with her awhile, as was his practice, alert to any sign of sleepiness within himself, anticipating none. A stick of Persephone's Pomegranate smouldered in a dish by the bed. Hannah twitched, opened her eyes to confirm that he was still there, twitched again and went peaceful.

Trev eased himself out of bed. As he passed through the living room the stench hit him again, signifying not sewage any longer but corrupted flesh, not life's shameful byprod-uct but its shameful end. In the bathroom, boxer-shorted and armed with a scrap of copper pipe from under the sink, he set to work. He drove the pipe through the drywall in a few spots, then whacked away until a chunk came loose. It was loud work, and louder again when the dust set him violently coughing, but no matter. This was the extra loneliness and liberty of living with a deaf woman. Out of sight, everything you did was clandestine, traitorous.

Halfway down the first stretch of wall Trev's jabbing encountered resistance. What he eventually worked free of the stud space was a doll, time-capsuled there (he also unearthed a yellowed newspaper from 1970, "Four Students Shot Dead at Kent State Campus") by whoever had built or renovated the bathroom. A blonde toddler in a party dress, the doll blinked her blue eyes up at Trev when he tipped her over, gamely swung her arms and legs. There was a little ring hanging from the back of her neck. Trev pulled it.

Please brush my hair, said the doll. Her voice was that of a woman mimicking the voice of a little girl. Trev pulled again.

I'm hungry.

Trev caught sight of himself in the mirror above the sink, a filthy hooligan clasping a little girl roughly in his arms.

Where are we going? she asked.

Trev dusted her off, slapped at his own hair a few times. In the bedroom he found Hannah propped up on her pillow, squinting in the light of the lamp she'd apparently just switched on. So something had reached her after all. A vibration, a waft of drywall dust. Or something from within, a rat dream, a rat vision.

Trev sat on the edge of the bed, baby doll in his lap. "I found her in the wall," he explained, and mimed his demolition procedure. He coughed, straightened the little girl's dress, fluffed up her synthetic hair. He pulled her string.

May I have a cookie?

Trev signed it for Hannah, who smiled and apologized that she didn't have one.

I hurt myself.

"Poor dear," signed Hannah.

Tell me a story.

Hannah frowned, then flipped back the bedding, patted the mattress beside her. Trev gave himself another dust off and climbed in, tucking the doll between them.

"Once upon a time ..." Hannah paused, her hands in the air above them, two bats frozen in flight. They began to dart about again. "Once upon a time there was a prince who lost his sight. It was the king, his father, who stole his sight from him. No, not his father. An imposter who'd drowned his father and taken his place."

Trev pulled the doll's string. *I love you*, she said. Trev translated it.

Hannah pressed her cheek briefly to the smudgy cheek of the doll, and went on with her story. "Late one night, when he couldn't sleep, the prince felt his way through the castle up to the very highest tower, the chamber of the royal magician. The prince asked the royal magician, What do I have to do so I can see again?"

Will you brush my hair? said the little girl. Trev left it untranslated.

"The royal magician told him, You have to do four things." Hannah paused once more, pondering. "First, you have to forget your name, and keep it forgotten."

Trev nodded, and caused the little girl to nod too.

"Then you have to remember what your mum used to call you when you were a baby. Way too young to remember."

The little girl's eyes were closed. Trev fought to keep his own eyelids up.

"Third, you have to do something else. You invent it, Trev, I'm out of ideas."

Let's have a party, said the little girl.

"Wait, I've got it." Hannah's hands were in motion again. "You have to picture everything you saw when you could see. You have to picture buildings and beaches."

Trev tucked the little girl in tighter.

"You have to picture hummingbirds. Ceiling fans."

Trev's eyes opened, fluttered shut, briefly opened again.

"You have to picture every single shade of red, and there are an infinite ... of Nelson Mandela where he's ... with jam, and another one with ... to picture a polar bear through the bars of ... a stem bent but ... blue water blue as ..."

It still existed, Hannah's voice, hovered in the heavy air. You didn't need to see it to believe it.

Via Negativa

I'm writing to follow up on today's (rather fraught!) family meeting. I apologize if I seemed brusque, which I imagine I did since I was brusque. My gratitude for the care you and your staff give my husband is beyond my ability to articulate it. That's as close as I'm going to get.

My husband, too, is clearly overwhelmed by what's going on inside him, and stymied when he tries to give it expression. You mentioned that yesterday Mario "took a swing" at somebody (I'm guessing it was Mrs. Prendergast?) who showed too much interest in his brownie. Let me assure you that Mario has never taken a swing at anybody in his life, certainly not in the twelve years I've known him. He's a pacifist, tender to a fault. People, including our two young kids, hide their suffering from him in order not to see him suffer.

Should I put all this in the past tense? Is Mario a different man, since the accident? I see no point entertaining this question.

You reported, rather puffily it seems to me, that you've managed to get Mario to stop swearing. No such luck getting Mr. Wallace to stop shouting "steeeerike!" every minute or so all day long, I notice, or in coaxing the bald lady (can't think of her name) to quit lecturing us on the evils of teeth. Apart from the plaque by the security keypad, there's been little overt evidence of the facility's "healing ministry of Jesus Christ," and for this I'm grateful. Is there something a little pious, though, about your obsession with profanity?

As you're aware, Mario's go-to curse nowadays is "holy fuck shit." Am I the only one to admire the efficiency of this transgression against the three big taboos, the religious, the sexual and the excretory? I understand that this phrase, and even more so the recent "mother fuck Christ whore," must be hard for the more delicate members of your staff. It's hard for me too, especially if Mario utters nothing else in the course of a visit.

But, as I argued at the meeting, I believe Mario should be allowed, indeed encouraged, to resume swearing. I apologize for the way I put it ("assface" is a term to which I rarely have recourse), but I feel strongly about this. You've argued that his cursing is a "cognitive distortion," that it has a "catastrophising" impact on him, locking him into an unduly negative and passive relationship with his condition. But this is nonsense.

Cursing kills pain. It's been demonstrated (I looked it up) that softening a curse deprives it of its analgesic power. Replacing Mario's "fuck" with "fudge" is like replacing his oxycodone with aspirin. I'd take a swing at somebody too.

What can happen to a person is beyond bearing. Religious types have said it, and now my husband's saying it, or at least he's making the attempt. Think of it as a religious path, a *via negativa* (another thing I looked up). Imagine that Mario's working his way towards the divine by itemizing all the things that aren't God. *Neti neti*, as the people in India apparently say. Fuck this, fuck that.

Will there be anything left when he's done? How should I know?

When I put the older of our two boys to bed tonight he asked me, "How can Mario's leg still hurt when it isn't there anymore?" My husband's never wanted to be "Dad" or "Daddy" to the boys, don't ask me why. Anyhow, I had no good answer for him, but it's occurred to me since that phantom pain is almost the paradigm of suffering. Pain is the physical expression of loss. Pain is our absence assembling itself inside us. "His body is lonesome for its leg." That would've been good. Why can I never think of the right thing to say at the time?

For instance, rather than telling you to "screw yourself sideways" today I should have said, "Recall that the word 'excruciating' comes from the cross, from crucifixion. Recall that even Jesus lashed out after a few hours up there."

Yes, lonely. So fucking lonely. Can you feel it, the way that "fucking" expands, releases?

You've had a long tough day, what with people like me. Why not give it a try? Just say it.

Pulse

Story about a guy who, inspired by the samurai thing of summing up life in a poem at the moment of death, wants to do that. But not a poem.

How will he know he's about to die? Has to assume he always is?

Symbols of impermanence: cherry blossoms, lightning, moon in a dewdrop. But something better, something contemp.

Setting?

"The point of all speech is silence." He reads this, make up where. He plans to turn it around, let silence speak. Dead Man Talking – title?

In Japan they used to do a haiku. He's going to tweet. How does he build up followers?

He doesn't want to write anything till he dies, but somehow he has to get people listening so there's a point. Or does he? Explore.

Don't include the death-tweet. Reader should be able to imagine it himself once he's read the story. Or she – make sure there's

A samurai had another samurai behind him to cut off his head when the poem was done. Our guy (name?) has to come up with something.

Hooks up a heart monitor to headphones so he can hear his pulse every minute of every day.

Yes, and he sends out his tweet between when his heart stops and when there's no him. #lastbeat

His father died suddenly of a heart attack, and his grandfather. What were they thinking, feeling? Idea that we'll never know.

Poe, Tell-Tale Heart. Unreliable narrator?

Creates an alternate persona to get famous first. Or could he get famous being himself, a man whose only ambition is not to say anything?

What about when he's asleep? The sudden silence of his heart not beating will wake him up.

Yes, the same way he used to wake up when his husband rolled over and stopped snoring.

So he had a husband. What happened to him? Left him for another man? For a woman? How not to specify which? Let the loss

The final moment, the one true moment, the moment that can't be revised. How to say this.

Come up with a new way of sounding out a heartbeat. Th-thump has been done to death. Use that line.

A lot of samurai cheated, wrote the death poem ahead of time. How will he resist this temptation?

Hearing his heartbeat changes him. At first drives him crazy, then something else.

Every novelist wants to write the last novel, the one that makes all other novels unnecessary, impossible. He wants to do this with Twitter.

Ryan?

An identity begins to form around the phony tweets. Is this his real self? When his heart stops beating, who will die?

Or characters, plural. What if he creates 140 characters through tweets of 140 characters? Self-reference. Find that book, the white one.

Jacob. Or is he Japanese?

How hard it is to keep saying nothing, even if you think nothing is the thing to say.

Darjeeling

Thank you all for being here today. As most of you know I'm Sara, Gail's daughter. My brother and I have so appreciated your condolences, and the memories of Mum you've shared with us, and we're honoured that you've joined us for this celebration of life.

But celebration of whose life, is my question. The woman who died on Monday wasn't the real Gail White. A lot of folks have been saying that. A lot of *you* folks, actually. The real Gail White was a smart, breezy woman, "a social butterfly with this crazy-smart brain," like her old friend Mrs. Hecht put it – hi Mrs. Hecht! – whereas the Gail White who died on Monday was, let's face it, I'm sorry but kind of dim. She kept moseying around in her old-womany sort of way, and she kept on talking, but she didn't have much to say, did she? Let's be honest. And she almost never knew who she was talking to. Just before she died she called out to me, "Not that one, the burgundy one!" referring to who knows what, whereas shouldn't she have been saying how much she loved me, how proud she was of me and my life? You've all been feeling bereft too, of course. You mourn the old Gail White, the real one. One of Mum's caregivers – okay, it was Marie – put a hand on my arm the other day while somebody was changing Mum's diaper and said, "Don't worry, this isn't your mother." She meant it kindly, but what about the woman having her bottom wiped? Who was that if not my mum? And where was my mum if she wasn't there having her bottom wiped? Of course I'd have been happy to hear how much my mother adored me, but if she wanted the burgundy one wasn't that her business?

I told Marie to go to hell, and that's kind of what I'd like to say to you folks too. Even you, Mrs. Hecht, though I know you and Mum go way back, to grade three is it? But do you really get to decide which was the real Gail White? Isn't that cruel? I should know, because Mum did it to me for years, for decades. I wouldn't be saying this except it's true. Mum got hold of one me, the me of about twelve years old, just before I got all sullen and spotty and started letting Davey Fry from youth group feel me up, sorry, and from then on she made sure I knew how disappointed she was in every new version of me. She kept it up till just after her second stroke, which you probably think of as when she started bursting out in song all the time, mostly sea shanties she'd learned as a young woman from her first serious boyfriend, Willie something-or-other, which was awkward since Dad had only been dead a month or so when she started singing, but to me the big thing was that she couldn't hang onto a real me anymore. She had no choice but to love the me standing in front of her. The actual me as opposed to the real me, if that makes any sense.

I know I'm going to regret saying all this, but so what? The me who regrets it won't be the real me, and neither is this one. How can I be the real me if I'm motherless? Motherless. Motherless. How can you be the same person you were when you had a sister or an aunt or a friend or whatever you lost when you lost Mum? What if you're in a coma right now, dreaming all this while Mum's alive and having afternoon tea, Darjeeling with a splash of homo? Or what if she's dead and you're here acting peculiar and don't know it? For instance, I got drunk on Mum's vermouth last night and fooled around on her couch with my high school boyfriend, who for some bizarre reason still lives in the old neighbourhood – hey Jason! – but was that the real me? Who exactly was Jason groping?

Sorry. I'm really sorry … What? Oh yeah, my brother and I hope you'll join us for refreshments and chat in the reception room, right through those doors. Those doors right there, just go through them.

The Rule and Exercises
of Holy Dying

I'm like, I bought the dress. The green one? Remember I said it was that or the black? You're gonna like it. You're gonna love it.

He's like, Oh.

I'm like, Hailey booked the limo. It's her and Ty and me and you. We'll do some shots here first. Mum and Dad have swing dance, ell-oh-ell.

He's like, Our life is but a vapour.

I'm like, What?

He's like, Thou cannot have a word that can signify a verier nothing.

I'm like, Not this shit again. Seriously, Brett, don't start.

He's like, He that would die well must always look for death, every day knocking at the gates of the grave.

I'm like, Do not, repeat, do *not* do this to me. The prom is in three days. I swear to God –

He's like, I have read of a young Eremite who –

I'm like, You must be kidding me.

He's like, I have read of a young Eremite who –

I'm like, What's a fricking *Eremite?* Do you even know?

He's like, Who, being passionately in love with a young lady, could not by all the arts of religion and mortification suppress the trouble of that fancy, till at last being told that she was dead, and had been buried about fourteen days –

I'm like, You're making me sick, Brett. Honestly, I'm gonna hurl.

He's like, He went secretly to her vault, and with the skirt of his mantle wiped the moisture from the carcass, and still at the return of his temptation laid it before him, saying, Behold, this is the beauty of the woman thou didst so much desire: and so the man found his cure.

I'm like, Is this you being deep and mysterious, Brett? Is that what this is? Because it's been done.

He's like, By who? By Cole? Is Cole deep and mysterious?

I'm like, I'm gonna go kill myself now, Brett. My mum has pills. Bye.

He's like, A man goes off and is forgotten like the dream of a distracted person.

I'm like, I saved myself for you, you know that? For Friday night. It was gonna be a surprise. Me and Hailey got a motel room. We were gonna take turns, them and then us. We flipped for it.

He's like, What about Cole?

I'm like, That was one blowie, Brett. One little blowie when I was wasted in the back of his mother's stupid Acura.

Which isn't the same, and which you wouldn't even know about if he wasn't such a Facebook slut.

He's like, Cole said two. Two blowies, and he had his finger inside you.

I'm like, And what have you had inside Shannon, hmm?

He's like, I have seen a Rose newly springing from the clefts of its hood, and at first it was fair as the Morning –

I'm like, I swear to God, Brett. I want to be with you. I'm saying … do you hear what I'm saying?

He's like, I'm trying.

I'm like, It's green. And silky. Feel it in your head.

He's like, Certain it is that a mourning spirit and an afflicted body are great instruments of reconciling God to a sinner.

I'm like, Are you going to start up with this crap on Friday night?

He's like, I don't think so.

I'm like, Because I can change my mind.

He's like, He that would die holily and happily must in this world love tears, humility, solitude and repentance.

I'm like, Half past seven. Gardenias, hint hint.

The Works

A buzzer sounds in the brimstone works, a brief, nerve-shredding racket, the kind of abject bleating sound a fire alarm might make if it were genuinely terrified of the flames. An infinite number of men down picks and shovels, make their way up the various tunnels towards the cafeteria and the vast phalanx of vending machines.

"Jeezuz aitch keeryst," mutters Franklin as he joins his buddies at their regular table. He grips a Styrofoam cup in one knobby pincer of a hand, a Twinkie in the other. His flesh smokes and sizzles as it cools in the stale air. "I thought that goddamn morning would never ... Hey, that's my chair. That one there, the one you're sitting in. How 'bout you get the fuck outta my chair?"

"What do you mean, *your* chair," says Stretch DeVries. "It's a *chair*, is what it is. One's the same as another." Stretch's nickname is well earned. Where other men shrivel in the heat of the works, bits of dung or dried fruit, Stretch elongates like pulled taffy. He's all limb, his torso a knot at the hub of his pipe cleaner physique. He squats on the chair in question like a spider on a dying bug, gazing querulously at the floor.

Franklin takes a deep breath, scowling for the billionth time at the scent of burnt flesh in his nostrils. He swivels his charred skull in the direction of one of the other men. "Al," he says, "Al, I don't think chairs are all the same. I really don't. What's your view?"

"Franky," says Al, placing the grey ember of a fingertip ruminatively on his chin, "I believe every chair's different, in this whole godforsaken world." He glances about in search of testimony, squinting against the bright sulfurous light. "Look, some have arms on 'em, some don't. That one has a gouge out of it just here, this other one –"

"So how 'bout it, Stretch?" says Franklin. "How 'bout you shift your ass outta there before this thing melts on me?" He dangles his Twinkie aloft so everyone can witness the moist chocolate pooling in pockets of the cellophane bag. The cellophane itself softens and elongates between his smouldering fingers.

Stretch sighs and grimaces, unfolds his legs and heaves himself onto another chair. Franklin slaps himself down.

There's a crackling in the air and a voice booms from the vast chasm above the men's heads. "Attention please. There will be a meeting of Local 196 in the upper lounge at eight o'clock tonight. This week's Wednesday night film will be screened on Thursday night instead. Thank you." The sound system cuts out with a deafening pop.

"Figure we'll strike, Franky?" says Al.

"Fuckin' right we'll strike," says Franklin. "And watch this place go to hell without us. I've forgotten more about brimstone than those bozos will ever —"

"They'll legislate us back," says Stretch, butting out his cigarette on the back of his hand.

"Nobody legislates me back to nothin'," says Franklin. He glares about at the other men at the table, inviting them to have a go at legislating him here and now.

"Medical and dental," says one of them.

"Buck an hour raise," says another.

"Goddamn rights," says Al. "Time-and-a-half for anything over twenty-four hours a day, or they can — Ah, shit." He whacks irritably at his head, which has burst into fresh flame.

Stretch raises his arms, coils them about himself in despair. "Time, time-and-a-half," he says, "what's the fucking difference? Don't you get it? We're here *forever*."

The other men stare at him blankly, so many chunks of charred furniture in a burned-out building.

"Well, fuck you then," Franklin finally offers, gnawing on his Twinkie. "Just f —"

Franklin's voice is obliterated by the back-to-work buzzer. He checks his watch, shakes his head. "I hate this goddamn job," he says. He's said it a billion times before, a billion billion, a billion billion billion, but for some reason he actually hears himself say it this time. "Huh," he adds.

Which is when Jesus appears, stumbling up out of one of the tunnels with a dismayed, nobody-tells-me-nothin' look on his face.

Everybody stares at him.

Jesus says, "Blessed is the one who came into being before he came into being."

"What the fuck are you on about now?" says Al.

Jesus says, "If your leaders say to you, 'Look, the kingdom is in the sky,' then the birds of the sky will precede you. If they say to you, 'It is in the sea,' then the fish will precede you. Rather, the kingdom is inside of you, and it is outside of you."

"Jeezuz aitch," says Franklin. He pushes himself to his feet, starts back down into the earth. Jesus turns and follows him.

Skeletal

She wasn't even going to do death, my daughter, or okay, step-daughter. She was going to do insomnia. Natalie's never been much of a sleeper, but it was worse than usual last week with her science project due and her having no plan. Her dad had the bright idea of using that – Tony was an actor when we first met (Nat was six at the time), and that's what actors do, use their own experiences to get into a part. Tony once played a guy whose wife switched gender and left him, and every night before he went on he'd remember his best friend moving away to Europe when he was a kid, how that felt. He was pretty good. It makes me sad, all the things he and I used to do and now don't.

Anyhow, Nat was losing sleep over her project, so Tony said, "Why don't you *do* not sleeping?" Nat loved the idea. She pulled out her phone and looked up "what happens when you can't get to sleep," or at least that's what she intended to look up, but she only got as far as "what happens when ..." when the search engine filled in "you die." What happens when you die – it's a hard question not to want to see the answer to, especially when your favourite aunt is sick, which hers was, and still is, Tony's sister. And hopefully not but maybe dying. So that's what she touched on the screen.

Tony and I figured she'd be researching heaven and whatnot, so we started being open on that subject. Tony grew up Anglican, but a while ago he went Wiccan, mostly to be close to his sister. He explained to Nat that they believe in something called the Summerland, a meadowy sort of place you go to when you die. You hang out there for a while with people you've loved who're also dead, and then you're reborn.

"What were you last time?" said Nat.

"A lion tamer," said Tony. "No, I have no idea. You usually can't remember."

"Then how do you ...?"

Tony did his life's-a-mystery shrug. Nat came back with her eye-roll, which even if you've seen it before makes you think she's having a seizure.

"Have I ever told you about my Great-Uncle Alex?" I said. I explained that I couldn't say anything for sure about the afterlife, but that I once had a whole conversation with my Great-Uncle Alex about his business trips to the Middle East, even though he'd been dead three months. I was on mescaline that night, and I explained this to Nat – Tony and I have decided to keep going with the honesty thing even if, at times, it seems like a really awful idea.

"Mescaline?"

"A drug. Kind of like acid. Which I did too, I'm afraid, back when I was a singer."

"You didn't like it?"

"I loved it."

Tony said, "We should go to the Middle East sometime. Israel, Palestine. The three of us. Maybe once you've studied it in school."

"We've studied it," said Nat. "But is that actually what you'd talk about if you were dead? The stupid places you went to when you were alive?"

I tried to think back. "He talked a lot about camels," I said. "And the wind, this hot wind, how it was like the planet was gasping for air. Or I might be making that part up."

As it turns out, Nat's project wasn't about this kind of stuff anyhow. Her project was about maggots. Microbes and maggots. What she wanted to know was what consumes us, and what happens to us as we're consumed. For her presentation she made five life-sized cutouts of herself, having me trace her on a big role of brown paper. I didn't angle the marker in to make her look less chubby – the honesty thing again. Then she got out her water colours and painted what she'd look like at each of the five stages of decomposition.

She sang to herself the whole time she was painting, some obnoxious new song, *do me n-n-n-n-now*. I sang along, even threw in a bit of harmony, but Tony was bugged as usual by the lewd lyrics from his little girl so he kept interrupting to ask about the stages. Fresh, for instance, the very first. Nat just looked like herself at this stage, or her own goofy rendering of herself, but she explained to us that her blood was pooling, her muscles were stiffening, and her body was beginning to digest itself. Autolysis – she hand-wrote a glossary on a separate sheet of construction paper. And then Bloat, for which she had to do shading to show her belly ballooning out from the gas given off by the microbes going crazy in there, which also forced purple (in Nat's version) liquid out from here and there. And then Active Decay, when the maggots really got going. Nat isn't much of an artist, fortunately, but that one was still disgusting.

"Maggots are just baby flies," said Nat. "And babies are cute." Tony's face was doing that funny-ugly thing where he might cry, so I got into it with Natalie about the maggots. It's a resolution of mine, to make myself see them the way she does.

Nat got an A+ on her project, but also a note that said we should come in for a sit-down with Mr. Okamura to discuss certain "issues" regarding her attitude. All five Nats are up on her bedroom wall now, taped over her other posters, which are of angry-looking women with tattoos and great tits and tight abs. Another issue awaiting us, I suppose. Below each Nat is the name of the stage she's on.

It was Tony who pointed out that there are five stages of decomposition and also five stages of grief (he's been preparing, even though he knows you can't), and they sort of line up. The first stage of decomposition is Fresh, for instance, and the first stage of grief is Denial, which is perfect. The second stage of decomposition is Bloat, and the second stage of grief is Anger. It goes on like that till you get to the last stage of decomposition, Skeletal (Nat's best painting, an x-ray on magic mushrooms), which lines up with Acceptance. Basically the survivor running out of misery just as the dead person runs out of flesh.

What's odd is that Nat's suddenly sleeping. Three nights in a row she's gone off at a decent hour and not come back. And I can kind of see it. If she were eaten she wouldn't be off there alone anymore, separate from her mum (the self-absorbed bitch) and her dad and her stepmum and her aunt and her friends and the branch scratching at her window and the window itself and the sand the window's made of, if that's actually how it works. Just thinking about it I can feel the day's dread start to seep out of me, a purple ooze.

Tonight, Tony comes back in from peeking at Nat. He nods – she's still asleep. I take his hand and bite it, the meaty bit, the bit you pound down with when you want to make a point. Tony howls, play-whaps me. I bite him again, on the shoulder this time, and he bites me back, and so on.

Sunday Morning

Theresa could normally be counted on to ignore a person's birthday, or at least to ignore the invitation to wish him or her a happy one on "sociopathic media," as she called it. She delivered this quip each time with a chagrined shake of the head, at her own anemic humour and the fearfulness it barely camouflaged.

Simon! she wrote in the little text box. She was sitting up in bed with the tablet Manny had given her for her last birthday. Morning light eased itself in between the honeycomb blinds. Manny slumbered beside her, his apnea machine giving out a rhythmical wheeze. *If you're getting older, I suppose I must be too!!* She couldn't bring herself to insert a smiley or a sad or a startled face. She aimed to make up for this deficit with a profusion of exclamation marks. *Have a whale of a day!!!!* Without once reading this over she tapped "enter," and nodded.

Manny breathed. He breathed again. Whale of a day? What had possessed her? What about her policy to tackle absolutely nothing until she'd got at least one cup of matcha down her in the morning?

It had been two decades since she'd last seen Simon. Three. Their only contact since then had been her click of the "confirm" button in response to his friend request. She imagined such a request to be prelude to further communication, but no. Even back in the day, Simon hadn't been anybody much to her. A coworker – she chewed gum at the checkout at Loblaws for a couple of summers, while he stocked shelves – and, briefly, a crush. Simon was a bona fide activist, as Theresa then aspired to be. She managed to get a letter to the editor printed, decrying the humpback hunt, at about the same time Simon nearly got himself harpooned on an inflatable boat in the North Pacific. And then there was that trace of a French Canadian accent – odd, when he'd grown up in Toronto. There was a short period, between her first two boyfriends, during which Theresa regularly masturbated to the sound of Simon's voice in her head.

Speaking of which, it had been too long, weeks at least, since she'd last "pleasured" herself. Dr. Leblanc, employing this icky euphemism or even, as he explained, going francophone slang on her – "tu te crosse, oui?" – urged her to persist in order to "keep the flow" while Manny sorted out his erectile issues. Maybe today, once Manny was off to see his daughter. Maybe with Simon in mind.

How would he look these days? Where his picture ought to be, at the top of his page, there was only a shot of his hand, buried in the coat of a spaniel. It was a lean hand, strong but delicate, mapped with veins as though fresh from some exertion. This hand might do.

Theresa scrolled down a bit. Others had already done their duty this morning – it must be a daily chore for habitual users, felicitating somebody or other. Simon seemed to have racked up 561 friends, so a good ten birthdays a week. Mind you, there must be others who, like Theresa, had declined to admit to having been born on any particular day. *Miss you my friend, wish I could crack you a cold one wherever you are.* Ah, so still a travelling man. Down the page a little further, *Hope your blowing a joint with Bob Marley right now #onelove.* Had he turned rasta? Sunk even further into his idealism, failed to mature? And then, *Two years, my sweet, since that dreadful day. I knew nothing would be the same. Nothing is.*

Oh.

She scrolled down further, and further again. Simon's last post was indeed from about two years back. *I don't usually inflict this kind of thing on you folks but i'm a sucker for this one ha ha prost santé cin cin cheers.* Followed by a video of an octopus uncorking a bottle of Veuve Clicquot. Either Simon didn't know his life was almost over at the time, or he'd so transcended his egotism, his sense of himself as a uniquely precious and irreplaceable being, that he could carry on unfazed.

But seriously, what the fuck? The infernal thing kept sending out birthday reminders even after a person had snuffed it? Manny would get a kick out of that. It would confirm something or other for him, and he loved to have things confirmed. Then again, who didn't? Theresa would share the story, starting out in a comical vein but modulating to sadness, and then maybe back again. She'd make it about technology, but about mortality too. Was the failure of the body actually a death at all, if the self continued to find means, however grotesque, of becoming manifest in other lives?

She sat up hard, sending a decent little shudder through the bed. She coughed a couple of times. Manny stirred, but resettled.

Oh well. She scrolled upwards, looking for more clues. From the comments, she couldn't ascertain how Simon had died, which didn't seem a good thing. The sheer plenty and variety of his friends instantly caused her to perceive her life as small and lacking in meaningful consequence. This tended to be the impact of online experience, whenever she got up the gumption to sign on to something. She'd get a little rush of fellow feeling, followed almost immediately by a great unaccustomed loneliness.

Another friend of Simon's had chimed in now, up at the top of the page. *Omg some people.* Aimed at her, presumably. And another, *How bout some effin respect.* Oh dear. She must appear ignorant, insensitive. Was there any way to revise this impression? Should she bother? She once again clicked the "Write something to Simon ..." box, noting beside it her tiny portrait. In her blue crew-neck sweater, she laughed and looked off to one side, such that she almost seemed to have a cheekbone again, unblurred by recent accretions of flesh. She recalled the day Manny lucked into this shot, even recalled what had amused her, or almost recalled it. They'd been to the Picasso exhibit, the one structured around his various muses. Their friends Pete and Saul had been along. Saul had wisecracked that "muse" meant "somebody an artist bonks, or hopes to." Pete had tossed in something about Cubism and sadism, and then Saul had tried to piece together a joke he'd heard about a model posing, not for Picasso, but for that guy who did the big blocks of colour. No, it wouldn't quite come back. Unless that was it, unless that was the whole joke?

Life gives you things for a while, Theresa tapped out on her tablet. *Then it starts to take them away again.* Cliché, and not true to her state of mind at the moment. Delete delete delete. She gave another couple of coughs, but still Manny puffed peacefully away. She'd come to love it, the look of him in his apnea mask. He wanted to be well. He wanted to be with her.

Rothko. Mark Rothko.

When I think about you, Simon, je me crosse. He'd be familiar with the Québécois expression, surely. And who knows, her little nudge might make him feel better about having perished. *As for the rest of you, I don't think about you at all.*

Enter. There. Too late.

Monsters

There are errors in her note, fine points I wish I could take up with her now. For instance, she claims it was Thomas Aquinas who taught that unbaptized babies will spend eternity in hell, and Augustine who taught that they won't. It's actually the other way around. According to Thomas Aquinas, unbaptized babies such as our Caitlin will never attain supernatural happiness, having died in original sin, but neither will they be subjected to unending punishment. They'll be barred from the bliss of the beatific vision, but they won't know there's any such thing, so the lack won't torment them. They may even be eligible for some sort of rudimentary peace.

Also, when I said I wished I could rip the faith right out of her heart, it wasn't her faith in us I was trying to steal, but her faith in the men who think they know the universe and our place in it. When I offered, as an alternate religious view, that of the Wari people who liberated their dead babies by eating them, it wasn't to deepen her horror at our loss but to shake her faith in faith itself. It didn't work. It was a bad idea.

She ended her note with hope more than faith, and for this I wish I could express my admiration. Express it to her, I mean. The modern church, she argued – her note is three pages long, written in the same lean script in which she used to write "avocados 3" or "tired hon hitting the hay night night" – took a hopeful view of both unbaptized babies and suicides. There was no way to be sure God would spare either from eternal damnation, but there were grounds to imagine He might. Caitlin almost certainly wasn't in heaven, but she wasn't necessarily in hell either. By killing herself, my wife gave herself a shot at joining our daughter in the indeterminate nothingness to which she'd been consigned. I'd book my own place in the lake of unquenchable fire if I could be assured that it worked, that the two of them are together and okay.

Hope, yes, and mercy. Her note bears no trace of resentment for my standing in the way of our daughter's baptism, my insistence that we wait at least until she'd healed from the first surgery. I'd have found another excuse after that – I'd never have consented to a baptism, or to any such rite I knew to be nonsense, and my wife recognized this. But again, her words betray no ill will. This is where I'd perceive the supernatural, if I could be persuaded that such a thing exists. In my wife's ability to resist this rage.

And in Caitlin too, of course. How could something merely natural cause a man to love so helplessly, so irredeemably? With her sweet puzzled face and her organs bulging out through the wall of her belly she was sublime, and monstrous. Monstrous in the sense of the medievals who traced such deformity to the wrath of God, or to the unclean bodies of women. Perhaps I'm the one who should feel aggrieved. Did my wife make brutish love to me while she was menstruating? Did she conceive our girl while she had some silly or unsettling notion in her head? "It is not good that monsters live among us," observed Ambroise Paré in the sixteenth century, for, entering a woman's overheated imagination, any such disturbance may "spoil the fruit" of her pregnancy.

He was right. Monsters – men like him, men like me – should be extinguished. Silenced, at least, before we can do any further damage. Men who think we know more than we do, which is not a thing.

10 Things

To Mr. Pearce,

This note will be longer than it ought to be. Hopefully you'll
live long enough to finish reading it, ha, ha. Is it right to joke
around? I don't know. I've looked it up, but nothing definitive.

My plan was to find the perfect card and let it do the
talking, let it express this peculiar grief. It's been almost
twenty years, after all, and we knew one another only slightly.
There was no "Sorry To Hear You're Dying!" section at the
shop, so I had to scout around. Trouble is, most cards have
a narrative to them, however subtle or implied. There was a
baby polar bear adrift on a chunk of ice, for instance. The
punchline, which I've now forgotten, was funny, but hinted
at lostness turning back into foundness. In other words, its
present implied a future, something of which you have very
little, I understand. (I've been back in touch with another

old student of yours, Owen McKnee. He'd somehow heard.) Any narrative at all is going to exclude you, correct? Carry on without you? The rest of us will be left behind too, someday. Does that make you feel better, or does it make you feel even worse?

So card-wise I was kind of hooped. I nearly settled for a cute cat one. A cat soaked down in the sink, a cat napping in a boot. Then I spotted a musical one, a blue autumn wind blowing ochre note-leaves over a treble clef. Appropriate (the melody looked as though it might be doable on the trombone, by somebody who'd absorbed your lessons), but it seemed to point in a too-heavy way towards silence. The narrative thing again. In the end, as you can see, I went geometric. This pattern reminds me of an early motherboard, the sort you'll see in a kicked-in old PC, but hopefully it reminds you of nothing. My idea was that the card wouldn't mean anything at all to you except, hey, this is a card.

Or should I say "To Robert," as though we met just recently instead of back when I was a kid and you were a man about the age I am now? Robert or Bob or whatever, and you'd call me Greg, just the way you did then. As in, "Sit up straight, Greg, so that the chest may fill like a bellows." (I was the skinny Italian-looking kid with the cheque-bouncing mother, by the way, in case you haven't placed me yet. Though I'm mostly Romanian.) It would be an exaggeration to say I think of you whenever I breathe, but you did change my attitude to the air that moves in and out of me, and I suspect there's nothing more fundamental. Mind and body are both breath, as it turns out. Perhaps that's why I'm writing this note and stuffing it into this card, instead of just planning to do so, which is more my style. You had a much bigger impact on me than you probably realize. And on Owen, and on a bunch of other kids too, I bet. All these little twerps dragged in for extra lessons, and you receiving us as though we mattered.

None of us wanted trombone, but you must have known that. If our parents were going to make us try out for school band, please God at least assign us something a little less dorky, trumpet or sax or something. We got stuck with trombone because we failed to hum "There's a Hole in My Bucket" as tunefully as some of our more gifted classmates. Which doesn't particularly make sense, since with its slide the trombone is so hard, notes never staying put. After a few months of lessons, though, out in the middle of "Ode to Joy" – blat blat blat blat blat blat blat, blat blat blat blat blat blaaaat blat – something happened. I felt it, and Owen says he felt it too. This sense of blowing our way into something bigger and more beautiful than us, or at least a little less small and ugly.

I bought you one other card, a "Congrats On Your Graduation!" one, which I thought would be funny. And I added a kind of cool quote. "He who has learned to die has unlearned to serve." That's Michel de Montaigne. I looked him up, which is worth it, though you probably already know about him. My hunch is that you've kept learning much longer than most of us, Mr. Pearce. But unlearning? It sounds hard. And really, is dying something you figure out how to do? The fact that you're dying doesn't mean you've learned how to do it, does it? Any more than falling out of an airplane means you've learned to skydive? Ms. Green from grade ten would be pleased with that metaphor, I like to think. Metaphor, is that what that is?

Anyway, I nixed the quote, and I nixed the clever card, which leaves me to come up with words of my own to slip into this motherboard. These words. As I say, I've made an effort. I've done some research. There are a lot of helpful sites, none of which are any help. "10 Things Not To Say To Your Dying Friend." You're going to a better place. You can beat this. Everything happens for a reason.

Here's a thing I read, though, on my ex's Facebook page (for some reason it's never occurred to her to unfriend me). She offered up this story sans emoticon or sappy commentary, which sort of singled it out. Seems there was an old Greek guy named Periander who wanted his body to disappear after he died. He arranged for two guys to kill and bury him. He arranged for four guys to kill and bury those two guys, and for eight guys to kill and bury those four guys. There may have been even more levels to it than that, I'm not sure. Another good metaphor for something, right?

I often feel stupid these days. Is it possible I'm unlearning things? In a good way, I mean? Unlearning to serve, to slave – that would be a worthy project. If anybody's up to it, if anybody's ever given me the impression it's something I might undertake, it would be you.

Thanks, Mr. Pearce. Robert. Bob.
Yours, Alex Petran

P.S. I'm going to come clean and confess that I don't play the bone anymore. I haven't since high school. Every so often I'll YouTube one of the classic jazz guys you had us listen to, Jack Teagarden, JJ Johnson, Dicky Wells. One time I dreamt I was playing again, searching out those tones and finding them. There wasn't any good reason for that dream to end.

P.P.S. No worries if you don't remember me. I'm not the point. I rarely am.

Coosh

The book in the outhouse said a person's last thought in this lifetime would dictate the kind of life they'd have next time around, how far up or down the Ladder of Being they'd go. This isn't what Ruth should be thinking about right now, here in bed. What she should be thinking about is Claire and her pleasure, only that. Claire is close. If Claire gets close but doesn't coosh (Claire's ridiculous but kind of cute term) it'll be a rough day for the both of them, especially since Ruth herself has already cooshed three times since noon when they crawled between these musty sheets together. Their relationship is only a few weeks old and it's already something of a pattern, Ruth for sure and then Claire maybe, maybe, maybe. It's partly just nerves — she's young, and this is her first serious thing with another woman — but still. Ruth needs to concentrate.

How far up the Ladder of Being, though, could one thought take you? How far down? The outhouse here at Claire's dad's cabin is disgusting, so Ruth didn't stick around to find out. The book was absent its cover, and absent its first fifty or so pages too. Could people really be wiping themselves with it? The TP was low today, and had clearly been nibbled by mice – Ruth herself thought of using the sacred text, which had English on one side of the page, Sanskrit or something on the other. There were *Archie* comics too, but these were intact. Out of bounds, apparently.

"*Ahh*-oh, ah-*ohh*." What's tricky with Claire is that her real noises sound so fake. If there were an orgasm ringtone it would sound like Claire cooshing, or in this case Claire thinking about maybe possibly cooshing sometime in the future. Ruth's losing ground. How about a little more ... yeah, like that. Tasty, Claire after a dunk in Clear Lake.

Justin? Jason? Claire's only mentioned her last boyfriend once, but she described him as "intense" and "spiritual" (implying the quotation marks, perhaps for Ruth's benefit), so the book may well be his. Why should this bother Ruth? Why should she care if Claire brought some guy here to her "heartplace" (as she described it on their way up this morning), if she sat with him on Reading Rock, jumped hand-in-hand with him off Silly Buggers Bridge? Why would it upset her to think of Jason in this same bed, his big ugly schlong between these same beautiful legs?

Hm. How far down the Ladder would that thought drop her? And it's true, Ruth could die right now, of course she could, not *la petite mort* but the big one. She's got that iffy valve in her heart, and she frets all the time about how much she frets, and about everything else too. So yeah, she could die, or she could fall asleep. That's always the most nervous part for Ruth, not the sex but the drifting off afterwards, which she's been able to avoid with Claire so far, claiming various early morning appointments as a reason not to stay over at Claire's place in town. But now the swim, the snack, the sex – how can a snooze not follow? And what will she blurt, once she's not awake to stop herself blurting it? Alia, Ruth's last lover, took to jotting things down and confronting her with them in the morning. "Close it!" she apparently cried out one night, "It's too yellow!" Alia wanted to know what was so yellow, and why Ruth was so keen to conceal it. But how could Ruth know that? How could she be held responsible for what went on in her own head?

Veronica. No, Betty. Which of them did Archie finally propose to, only then it turns out to be a fantasy and it's really the other way around?

Claire wriggles a bit, the more completely to reveal herself. *"Ahhhh. Ohhhh."* Better. More of that.

Yes. Betty and Veronica around back of Riverdale High, French kissing and feeling each other up – that may have been Ruth's very last fantasy before she jammed her tweezers into the outlet for the first time. Her little brother came along with their parents to be with her in emerg, and brought a stack of comics. Reggie and Betty, Archie and Veronica, boy-girl, boy-girl, how much time did she waste trying to have that fantasy instead? She's twenty-eight now, and it's just five years since the night she waded topless to the centre of the fountain at city hall and screamed *"Pussyyyyy!"* till her voice gave out. And here's Claire, stammering her way towards the same eruption at about the same age.

"Ah. Ah. Ah." Staccato, a promising sign. Ruth ups her intensity a touch, even as the drowsiness continues to build in her.

"Red rubber chicken, chrissake!" – Alia had to have been making that one up. But what will come out of Ruth today? And why is she worrying about Claire's reaction? A few weeks, can she really be this far gone?

"Ah-*oh*-ah-*oh*."

A good thought. How would you settle on one? How would you make yourself have it just as you drifted off, just as you died?

"Oh-*oh*-oh-*oh*-oh-*ohhh*...."

Not *I love you* yet but something even simpler, purer. Just *you?* Yes, and as she thinks it she speaks it too, deep into this delicious mouth, just *you you you.*

From the Journal of
Dr. Duncan MacDougall
of Haverhill, Mass.

October 18, 1906

Dispatched another dog upon the scale in the barn this morning, a mangy creature that had been molesting the Carleton flock. Got the dosage just right this time, such that the mutt was swiftly freed from its urge to struggle. Once again, the scale remained still at the moment of death.

It is virtually confirmed that a dog possesses no soul substance, which does not of course disburden me from the responsibility of seeing to its burial. Had I not a conscience of my own, I would rely on the figure of Mary lurking behind the muslin to supply that conscience for me.

Mutton for dinner, slightly overdone but tolerable.

October 19, 1906

Down to Dorchester to see the ranking physician at the sanitarium again, requesting just one more consumptive. He is unmoved.

Have elected to discard the results of Subject #4, the diabetic coma, because of the problem with the scales, and because of the actions of those meddlers who chanced to be present when he finally expired. Subject #6 also, the tubercular who passed before we were ready for him. This leaves four good subjects, though the first is still the most sound experimentally, and his loss of three fourths of an ounce at the moment of death our most reliable estimate of the weight of a soul.

October 20, 1906

Trouble with my lumbago again. Freed from the body, are we still capable of pain? So many questions yet.

October 21, 1906

Further to yesterday's thoughts, by what mechanism does the soul depart the body? Through what orifice, or by means of what emanation? What experiment might be designed to trace it?

Was offered a litter of puppies by the Johanson boy, but declined. My scale is, sadly, not sufficiently precise to register such a tiny soul. Besides, even a creature devoid of soul substance deserves its time upon the earth.

Lamb chops and the last of Mary's excellent mint jelly.

October 22, 1906

That the soul is not constituted of ether, and therefore weightless, can be deduced from the fact that the ether is continuous and not separable into discrete parcels, whereas the human being has separateness and aloneness as its most fundamental characteristic.

One more dog today, to firm up my results. A retriever, possibly purebred, with so-called "soulful" eyes. Ill, but not ill enough – injections were required. Again, the scale registered no alteration as the creature succumbed.

October 23, 1906

Patience, patience. Dr. L. has written to observe that at the moment of death the sphincter and the muscles of the pelvic floor relax, and that the sudden change in weight might therefore be explained by evacuations of urine and faeces. I have pointed out, with all due courtesy, that in none of my six cases was there motion of the bowels, and that anyway such evacuations would still be present upon the scale, as was the dram or two of urine each subject released.

October 24, 1906

"Hypothesis Concerning Soul Substance Together with Experimental Evidence of the Existence of Such Substance." Mary scoffs at my proposed title, as she scoffs at every manifestation of my research. It is not ignorance that holds her back, so it must be the greater flaw of stubbornness.

October 25, 1906

Presuming for a moment that a soul is the size of the body it inhabits, then at three fourths of an ounce a man-sized soul is less dense than the atmosphere which surrounds the earth, and will ascend without interruption.

Final draft off to the Society in today's mail.

October 26, 1906

The dream again, Subject #1 but somehow Mary too this time. Odd, because Subject #1 was of a far more phlegmatic temper than is my melancholic Mary. Where he took four hours to die she took but a minute, not long enough for me to convince her of the veracity of my theory, and thus to assure her that her death would not be a death. Awoke weeping for no reason.

October 27, 1906

Had another go at Mary after breakfast this morning. If a soul has not substance, what will transport a man from his dying body? Can emptiness bear upon itself a personality? Can nothing be something? Mary turned, silent, back to the kitchen sink, but I permit myself to believe I have made progress.

Back bacon from one of Carleton's hogs.

Centrifuge

Will pinched up his eyes as though to peer into his own head. "Cynth came to the door," he said. "No, it was a flap, I was in a tent. She wasn't dead, but she wasn't herself either. She was ... she was a raccoon."

Jorie made a listening face. It wasn't exactly a lie, she really was trying to listen. She tore open another packet of sugar and dumped it into her glass of water.

"Except more like an oil painting of a raccoon."

Jorie made her eyes go big.

Cynth had been gone two months. An overdose, probably accidental, though who really knew. This was the first time Jorie and Will had been together since the funeral, which Will described as the most depressing thing he'd ever experienced. Cynth's parents were Buddhist or something, sickeningly serene. They weren't Indigenous, but this didn't

john gould

stop them smudging everybody as they filed into the church. A guy with a piccolo played Beatles tunes as they filed back out. Will flipped him the bird.

"She opened her mouth," he went on, "and there was this choppy lake in there and suddenly I was swimming." His knee rhythmically hammered the underside of the table, corrugating the liquid in their glasses. "Then I remembered I can't swim, but actually I can, and I sank down into this pit that was a parking garage."

They'd agreed to meet at Cynth's favourite coffee shop, a scones-and-doilies sort of deal way out in the suburb where Cynth had grown up. Before she died, Cynth had worked out a way of sitting in this place that was so ironic that you couldn't even tell, she just seemed to be sitting there like an ordinary person. By the time Jorie arrived today, after a two-hour walk, Will had installed himself next to the only other customers in the place. He was kind of a prick that way – he was always trying to shake people up, mess with their notion of personal space, the whole idea that they got to set themselves apart. A prick, and a hero. His eye was still black and yellow from the time he took the urinal beside another dude when there were other urinals free.

"The garage had wallpaper with chipmunks sitting on branches," said Will. He ran his fingers over the scab on his forearm. Jorie tried to imagine that the scab was in the shape of something, but she couldn't think what. "Only instead of chipmunks there was something else. Organs, hearts. Like human hearts, at least I think they were human."

Jorie made the hummingbird tattoo on the back of her

hand dart and dip. She and Will had slept together once. His beard was gross, and he shook like a scolded dog the whole time, but he was oddly patient and kind. And of course they were both friends with Cynth, and believed her to be the best person they'd ever met. What else did they have in common? They both lived with their dads, there was that. Both dads wanted them out.

"The priest told us to turn to the hymn on page seventy-three." Will used his teeth to tear open a packet of crackers and set about smearing them with ketchup. "But my copy didn't have a page seventy-three so I had to come up with something."

After the funeral, Jorie had gone around back of the church and cried until she almost passed out. What had gutted her was a poem recited by Cynth's mother during the service. The poem was beautiful, and seemed to be known to everyone else. Not to Jorie. This fact brought on a sadness that went beyond what she could contain.

"The thing I thought of," said Will, "was that song from when we were little, 'Skiddy-mer-rink-a-doo.'"

He sang a bit of it, though the tune sounded wrong to Jorie. Then he went back to his monologue, pausing now and again to reconstruct another element of his dream. The people at the next table, a sniffy middle-aged couple who could hardly be imagined speaking to one another, were clearly failing not to follow along. Jorie couldn't sort out the headline on the man's newspaper because of the way he had it folded. "... Within Decade ... -ists Warn." Physicists? Dentists? Pianists?

"But the baby whale was bigger than the mother whale," Will was saying, "and it kept whistling and groaning in this lonely sort of –"

"Me too," said Jorie. "I had that dream too."

"What?" said Will. "Are you kidding me?"

"Nope." Imagine, if life actually worked that way. "I mean, not every detail. Like there was no centrifuge in mine. And Cynth was never Celine Dion. But mostly, yeah."

"Crazy. Just … crazy."

In the coming months, it became clear that Will was investing more and more significance in the shared dream. Whenever Jorie ran into him he expressed the belief that it linked the two of them to Cynth and to each other at a "sub-lingual" level. Not the right word, and Jorie felt good about leaving it be. She felt good, too, about the sense of communion she'd imparted to Will, though not so good that she'd done so with a lie. Did it matter?

Without exactly meaning to, she started to avoid Will, steer clear of his hangouts. She never did dream about Cynth, but when Will died, another overdose, she dreamed about him. She wrote the dream down, the bits of it she could remember – a spaceship made of stone, a room in which you had to keep counting all the corners or your hair would fall out – and tucked the slip of paper into the same old metal tea box in which she kept a bird bone and a photo of her mum and a few other things.

Sodom

Lot's daughter – the younger of the two virgins, she's about my age – says to me, "Why do you have to be so negative all the time?"

Our usual quarrel. Lot's daughter and I have been seeing each other on the sly for a while now (Lot would hit the roof), and she's annoyed by my bleak moods. Girls are drawn to brooding guys, but once they've got them they expect them to cheer up. This has been my experience.

I take another sip of goat's milk from my clay vessel. "It's the whole point of thought," I say. "Thought is inherently negative. Its whole purpose is to foresee catastrophe. That's why we started to think in the first place, so we'd be ready for what's about to go wrong."

"Are you breaking up with me?"

"See?" I say.

"See what? Oh, ha ha." She tears off a bit of unleavened bread, gnaws at it. Even this, even gnawing unleavened bread, is sublime when done by Lot's daughter. No one in his right mind would ever break up with this girl for any reason.

"Like I say," I say, "there's going to be fire and brimstone. Here in Sodom, and maybe in Gomorrah too. Raining, and I mean *raining* down on us. For one thing, we live in a serious earthquake zone. For another thing, the rocks around here are laced with flammable sulphur and bitumen. For one more thing, our sin is grievous."

Lot's daughter has been rolling her eyes the whole time, her beautiful tar-dark eyes. "You really are a gloomy gus, aren't you?" she says. She allows the back of her hand to brush my arm where it's bare beneath the sleeve of my tunic. I wish it were me with whom she'd one day stop being a virgin. I'm ready to stop being a virgin with her right here, right now, on the dirt floor of this hewn-stone building. My every desire is an abomination.

"God's angry," I say. "Why wouldn't he be? Here's what's going to happen. God's going to get angrier and angrier, and eventually He'll decide to destroy us. He'll send down men who'll turn out to be angels, probably two of them. Your dad will take them in, but a mob will surround the house and demand to be allowed to rape the angels."

"Rape the angels?" says Lot's daughter. "Yup, you're a laugh riot."

"But your dad won't give them the angels, he'll offer you and your sister to the mob instead. Two virgins in place of two angels. The mob will turn him down, but the angels will strike the mob blind so you and your sister and your parents can slip away before the rest of us burn to death. You'll escape, but you may wish you hadn't. Your mum will turn around and look back at the burning cities, which for some reason God will have told you not to do, and she'll turn into a pillar of salt."

"Pillar of salt," says Lot's daughter. She once called me a poet, but almost in a nice way.

"Pillar of salt," I say. I try to say it like poetry. "You and your sister and your dad will make it to a cave where you'll hide out together, imagining you're the only people left in all creation, and you'll get your dad drunk and have sex with him so you can be fruitful. Or that'll be the official version, but obviously the incest will be your dad's idea. You'll have a son by your father and name him Ben-Ammi, from whom will arise the Ammonites, a nomadic people who'll worship the god Moloch."

"Is this really the kind of stuff you think about all the time?" says Lot's daughter.

"Pretty much."

"What if you didn't?"

"Pardon?"

"Who says we have to think all the time? What if we didn't?"

"Didn't think?" I say. "You mean, like animals?" I have no idea whether or not animals think. Abisha, our ass, sometimes gets a look on his face you could call pensive, but what's really going on in there?

"Thinking and then not thinking is completely different than not thinking in the first place," says Lot's daughter.

"Interesting point." I refill our clay vessels.

"And hey, what if you came along with us?" She seems to have believed me, my tale. "I'll tell Dad I won't flee with him unless you can come too."

"That's sweet of you," I say. "I really appreciate it." Lot's uncle happens to be Abraham, the patriarch with whom God made the Covenant. Like he's going to marry his daughter off to me, the iniquitous son of some scribe.

Lot's daughter dips a piece of unleavened bread into her goat's milk. I want to be with her for the rest of my life, short and vain as it may be, watching her do little things like this.

I say, "How would we stop thinking?"

And what's odd is that just for a couple of seconds there, I do. I stop thinking, or at least I think that's what happens. Something about the question itself, the ruin that hasn't yet rained down on us, the darkness of Lot's daughter's eyes as she wonders what to say to me next. It's as though God has touched me, or maybe it's as though God has let me go.

Corkscrew

I don't go out of my way to watch violent shows on TV, but last night Suze fell asleep with her head in my lap and I couldn't reach the clicker. Her romance ended — the rich bloke thundered up on his steed, the lady loosened her bonnet — and on came an action movie called *Corkscrew*.

The hero of *Corkscrew* was a martial arts guy, a wiry little dude like me. When he first appeared he was running late for a picnic in the park with his girlfriend. The girlfriend was played by one of the actresses from the romance, not the main one but the supporting one, the one who'd played the rich bloke's snooty, meddlesome sister. This seemed an odd coincidence, but maybe it wasn't — maybe that's why the two movies were being run back-to-back in the first place.

It was a fine spring afternoon, light angling in through cherry blossoms, and the martial arts guy looked happy.

When he arrived at the park, though, there was something the matter with his girlfriend. She kissed him lovingly, but her breath came in little gasps. Before long her eyes went flat. He tried CPR on her, but no go. There she was stretched out on her sky-blue blanket, wicker basket splayed open to reveal the picnic gear, cutlery and plates and glasses and of course a corkscrew for the bottle of wine still chilling in its bucket of ice. Everything was perfect, except that she wasn't alive. This not-aliveness was clearly something that needed to be solved, or if not solved at least redressed.

The martial arts guy knew, as we did too if we'd paid attention during the opening sequence, that his girlfriend's death wasn't an accident but a murder, at the hands not of common thugs but of members of a drug cartel run by heavily-bearded men with Middle Eastern accents. After a brief, manly weep the martial arts guy took up the corkscrew, not as a memento, as we soon discovered, but as a weapon. Over the next ninety minutes or so – Suze was really crashed out after a long day at the hospital, topped off by the money fight we'd had over dinner, which I was pretty sure hadn't been about money – he employed it to put holes in a lot of people. I lost track, but a couple of dozen at least. I kept thinking he'd done everything he could possibly do with a corkscrew, punctured every vulnerable part of a person, but he'd always find another. Each death was more horrific than the last, and more gratifying too, as we gradually worked our way up the hierarchy of evil. I'm a nonviolent man, verging on wimpy, but by the end I loathed the main bad guy so much I'd have been happy to uncork him myself.

When Suze woke up, the romance was on again – they were apparently going to alternate the two movies all night long. This disconcerted her a touch, since she seemed to have woken up before she went to sleep, near the beginning of a movie she'd almost finished. Before I could explain, she started in about a dream she'd just had in which she'd been forced to operate on herself, the only instrument available to her being a corkscrew. It wasn't painful so much as bizarre to feel the steel penetrating deep into her chest. She just kept cranking, and finally drew out her heart with a satisfying pop. She watched it glow a while, then grow dim, dark. The darkness woke her up.

"Wow," I said.

"Yep."

How had the corkscrew image made it into her dream? Psychic stuff doesn't tend to reach me, but in this case I was intrigued. More than intrigued, I was kind of worked up about it, possibly on account of all the excess adrenaline in my system. Adrenaline from *Corkscrew*, tenderness from the romance.

"I'm done," said Suze. "Bedtime." She tried to sit up, but failed.

"Hey," I said. "When you were snoozing there, did you maybe wake up at some point? And see a guy with a corkscrew?"

"There was a corkscrew in *Spoons?*"

Spoons was her romance, its title inspired by the lady's pet image of conjugal bliss. I suppose that may have been the real reason the movies had been programmed as a pair, the utensil motif. "Or maybe you heard somebody say the word corkscrew?"

"Maybe."

But as I went over it in my mind, I grew more and more convinced that the word had never been spoken. Not by the cops, not even by the coroner, because that was part of the point, that everybody kept being mystified about the weapon.

"Okay, this is it," said Suze. After a few more tries and a boost from me she made it up out of my lap. "Goodnight." She kissed me on the neck.

"Goodnight." I should have said more, but what?

Then it was just me and the TV. I was starting to get the blood back into my legs (I'd been sitting funny, and Suze's head is not light) by joggling them as though I had a fussy baby in my lap. The baby question, was that what we'd actually been fighting about? Can you fight about something that simply scares and confuses you both? Or maybe it had been about our addictions, work (hers) or smoking (mine). It could have been about any number of things.

There was an hour or so of *Spoons* still to go, and then *Corkscrew* would come back on. Could I make it? I was suddenly desperate for proof. Proof that the image of the corkscrew had been transmitted directly to Suze's mind from mine. Proof that, recent troubles notwithstanding, our connection went that deep. Proof that there was something more to us than could be obliterated by poking us full of holes. As I say, I was worked up.

Spoons was better the second time around. I was more attentive to it, and more receptive, more in need of it after the ordeal of *Corkscrew*. I'm embarrassed to say how badly I wanted the couple to get together, how anxious I felt about it even though I'd already seen the movie through to the end. I knew they'd be happily united, yet I couldn't bear to see them apart. Action or romance, murder or marriage, either could grab and hold me, it seemed. Separation or union. Though actually, wasn't death a union too, since birth was a separation, and death the undoing of it? Why hadn't some of these deep thoughts come to me while Suze was still up so I could have shared them with her, got us talking again?

I must have been wearied by our fight too, I guess, and by the movie marathon, because at some point I fell asleep. When I woke up I found that I'd stretched myself out and half covered myself with cushions. *Corkscrew* was just ending for the second time. Everybody who had to die had done so. The martial arts guy released his bloody weapon into the river, which absorbed it with barely a ripple.

I turned off the tube and headed for bed. I could have stepped out for a cigarette first, but I didn't. I crawled in with Suze, cuddled up. I prepared myself to dream about whatever she had inside her.

Something Apart

Along with his prognosis – six months, maybe twelve – Dan's doctor offered him a piece of advice. Doctors tended to be young these days, alarmingly so, but this one was older than Dan by a good decade. Retirement age or even past it. He didn't exhibit the brisk, let's-do-business demeanor the young ones were affecting, but that of a hobo or addled genius. Karl Marx if Karl had indulged in a few more muffins.

"What matters?" said the doctor. "What have you always meant to do? Swim with the dolphins? Lick Château d'Yquem from your secretary's cleavage?"

Dan said, "I don't have a secretary."

"So, the dolphins. I'm saying, your pancreas? Forget it. Do the thing."

Do the thing. Decent advice. There were challenges, though. First, Dan couldn't bring to mind anything, or anything of any worth, he'd always meant to do. If there'd been such a thing he must have done it, or lost the ambition.

And then the problem of planning. The source of all anguish is time – such was the view of Kamilah, Dan's therapist. Kamilah regularly urged Dan to resist the fascism, as she put it, of past and future, to release himself into the present. "Time is nothing but tension," said a little plaque over Kamilah's chair, and under that, "Saint Augustine." It was a shiny plaque, in which Dan could study the back of Kamilah's head, her straight hair reflected wavy. He'd been seeing her for a year now, since a month or so after the Monique debacle, and despite Dan's scepticism her program showed signs of success. Whenever he felt particularly wrought up he'd begin silently to chant, *no past, no future, no past, no future. No past* on the in breath, *no future* on the out, *no past, no future*. Strolling of an afternoon he'd call to mind his lunch and his dinner, and demand of himself whether he could, at that moment, take a bite from either of them. He could not. Lunch did not exist, nor did dinner. Nothing existed but the benignly unmusical barking of a dog, the burn of the insipient blister on his heel. Reliably, this exercise bled the tension from Dan's body, opened his senses in a satisfying if slightly unsettling way.

So it was that he'd been living in the present, more or less, for the better part of a year. If he were to buy into his new doctor's well-meaning advice, this progress would be sacrificed. He'd have to look up dolphins, enquire as to where you could swim with them, make arrangements. He'd be reduced to the level of all the other lame bucket-listers, grasping at their humdrum dreams. Pass.

But then *Heart of Darkness*. Dan was doing a muck-out of his apartment, with no particular goal in mind – indeed with as little foresight, as little intent as he could muster – when he happened on his old copy. That familiar cover, a bald head shining bright as a light bulb but smeared with some kind of copper emulsion. And with coffee too – *Heart of Darkness* was pretty much the only Great Book Dan had ever read all the way through, and he'd read it all the way through half a dozen times in the months after he discovered it at school. It had been left behind by a student of literature or colonialism or some such, in the lecture hall in which Dan took his macro economics class. On his first date with his wife, Monique, a couple of years after this discovery, and about twenty-three years before the debacle, she gently boasted of the dream of reading Kafka in the original German. Dan countered with the dream of reading *Heart of Darkness* in "the unoriginal Spanish." Monique laughed at this way of twisting the thing around, giving voice to the wonky hunger for the strange. What surprised Dan was how long it took her to realize that this bit of absurd insight was an anomaly for him, no doubt induced by the fever of the moment, the surpassing intensity of his infatuation. In the normal course of things, he just wasn't that kind of clever.

Spanish. Well, he'd waited tables with a Guatemalan guy one summer, picked up a few phrases. Plus there were apps you could download. It would be a plan, but such a pointless one that it hardly seemed to count. Not so much spending time as willfully squandering it.

Nobody had a copy of *El corazón de las tinieblas* in stock. Four to six weeks, they said, but the book arrived in three. On the cover of this edition there was a still from the

Francis Ford Coppola film (loudly derided by Dan when it first came out, as evidence of his intimacy with the book), Marlon Brando peering through a pall of napalm smoke. There wasn't going to be time to read the whole thing, especially since Dan's Spanish comprehension had yet to rise to the level of a toddler. So, the end. Start at the end. Give the finger once again to time, to fate, to cause and effect. Six to twelve months? Fuck you.

Marlow calló, se sentó aparte, indistinto y silencioso, en la postura de un Buda meditando. Well, this was a bit of luck. Two names. Marlow, that was the main guy, the guy who went up the river in search of the dying madman. Why? What was the point of it? Did Dan ever get that sorted out? And the Buddha of course. A young woman at Dan's work used to wear a T-shirt, *Are you for real with this nonattachment shit?* And then the rotund little laughing guy, but with his head broken off, a shattered sculpture. That was the Buddha. Dan had told Monique about the T-shirt, and then forgotten he'd told her and told her again. "Nice tits, does she?" Monique had asked him.

The rest of the sentence came pretty easily too. Spanish looked a lot like English, actually. Were all languages essentially the same? Was there was no reason, down deep, for people to misunderstand one another? *Marlow something, something apart, indistinct and silent, in the pose of a Buddha meditating. Meditating Buddha* sounded better, for some reason. *In the pose of a meditating Buddha.*

He'd text it to Monique. Just like that, let her puzzle it out. Would she recall that moment, so many years ago, in the days before either of them was dying? She hadn't heard tell of his pancreas yet, he was holding that back, ace up his sleeve. He picked up his phone and tapped out, *Hola! It didn't happen, we didn't say or do what we did or said. If we had it would have been in the past and there isn't one.*

At his session with Kamilah the next day, Dan rehashed some of the old material, then filled her in on his text, and on Monique's answering silence. "I think I get it now," he said. "The whole impermanence thing."

Kamilah checked the clock on the wall behind him. Dan laughed and nodded, but no, his time really was up.

Party Game

The game was who would you sleep with if you could sleep with anybody. The person had to be real but not necessarily alive. You couldn't say Catwoman, for instance, but you could say Eartha Kitt, and you'd probably get some woo-hoos for it. Also, the person had to be famous – we added that after the time Andy chose Linh, Phil's wife, kind of joking but kind of not. He'd had maybe four red-headed sluts (peach schnapps, Jägermeister and grenadine over ice), and Phil took a swing at him, threw his shoulder out. No softball, no nothing for weeks.

So yeah, the person had to be famous. I'd always gone with living women, but this one time I couldn't think of anybody hot enough to be convincing but so-so enough to be safe. Pam had been funny with me ever since the night I said Julia Roberts, and that put me on my guard. Pam hadn't been bothered about any of my other choices – we'd been playing the game at our parties every couple of months for a couple of years – but Julia Roberts got to her. Maybe the mouth, Pam's got kind of an odd little mouth and of course Julia's is giant, but anyhow, we'd get the kids off to bed and start fooling around and Pam would throw in some wisecrack. I'd come back with Jake Gyllenhaal (she's been soft on him ever since that gay cowboy movie), but my heart was never in it. You invite a person to fantasize, do you really have the right to flip out about their fantasy?

Anyhow, this particular night I couldn't come up with anybody alive, so I blurted out Mary Mansfield.

"I think you mean *Jayne*, sweetie," said Pam. "It's *Jayne* Mansfield." The "sweetie" was promising, and she leaned over the coffee table and popped the olive from her old yeller (prune juice and whiskey) into my mouth.

"The girl can't help it," said Phil, this being, as I found out later, the name of a Mansfield movie. "Hot damn."

The thing is, I didn't even know who she was, Jayne Mansfield. I'd caught her name when the kids were watching a show counting down the top ten famous car accidents. Lady Di was tops, but Pam knew I'd actually had a thing for her at one point, so no. Everybody thought Jayne Mansfield was a good choice, the men because of her bombshell body, the women because she was smarter than people realized, smart enough to play the dumb blonde to her own advantage. To no one but me was it bizarre that I wanted to sleep with somebody dead.

Jayne came up again later in the evening. Linh said, "Wasn't she the one who got her head lopped off? Drove her car under a truck and ... shhht." She made as though to decapitate herself with the blade of her hand. Others poo-poo-ed this as an urban legend, and we got telling other urban legends (Mr. Rogers was a Navy SEAL, Lady Gaga has a dink) until babysitters started texting and we all went home.

That night Pam was in a big hurry to get to bed, Julia Roberts forgotten. It's likely she still had Daniel Day-Lewis on her mind (she's adored him ever since that gay laundromat movie), but anyhow she was pleasantly eager while I attended to her, and then zonked straight off to sleep. I slipped out of bed and went to look in on the kids. Then I poured myself another drink, and another. Eventually I nodded off on the couch.

Maybe it was the odd position I was in, my neck cranked around, but anyhow my dream turned weird. Jayne Mansfield was there on the couch with me, my version of Jayne Mansfield, a petite, Pam-like woman but with massive blonde hair. I remember the hair, so she definitely had a head, whereas I didn't. There was nothing where my head should have been, just a space filled up with the two of us. My being headless didn't bother us much, in fact quite the opposite. When I awoke I'd actually climaxed in my boxers, my first wet dream in many, many years.

After that it started happening when I was awake. Not the impromptu orgasms, but the sense of having been beheaded. I knew there was a head on my shoulders, I could see it in the mirror, but I was looking at it, not out of it. What would that even mean, to look *out of a head?* What kind of sick fantasy was that? No, there was nothing where the looking was going on, just all the stuff I was looking at. Once, when Pam and I first met, she got some amazing hash from her ex-boyfriend and we smoked it every couple of hours for a whole weekend. On Sunday afternoon we went down to the water and looked at the waves, and it was kind of like that. Just the waves, nothing else. No head for them to slosh around in.

I described it to Pam that way, after my first couple of episodes, and she remembered. "It was like the waves were licking me," she said. "Except not like that at all."

"Right, exactly," I said, though it seemed a peculiar way to put it.

"And it's happening again?" she said. "Like, when?"

"Just whenever." Which was true, I hadn't been able to discern any order to the incidents. "Once at work, when I was standing at the copier. Another time at home when I was doing the dishes. It was like the sink was where my head should be. Fantastic."

"And you weren't wasted or anything?"

"No."

"Are you worried?"

"Not really. A little."

What I didn't tell her was my Jayne Mansfield dream. Then I changed my mind and I told her. "But Jayne was you," I assured her, which was kind of true, as much as a person in a dream is anybody. "You with a big blonde wig."

"Perv," said Pam. The kids were at their cousins' place that night, so we did it right there on the couch, me and Pam. The thing is, I had a head the whole time.

After that I started keeping track of when I had a head and when I didn't. The only pattern I could make out was that the headless episodes were getting shorter and less frequent. One of my last ones was at another party. I was watching Pam eat peanuts, this finicky way she has where she gets one on her thumbnail and flicks it into her mouth. I was there at the party too, but then also not. There was a me who was at the party, alive and doing stuff like everybody else, but also a me who was different, dead or never born. Something like that.

Since then there've been a couple more, but nothing for a while. If I could get some of that hash, I'd smoke it. If I could get back into my dream with blonde Pam I'd slow it down, I'd take for fucking ever.

Project Description

Cupid, for which I am requesting a Level II grant (see attached form 3B), will be the final installment in my *bODYbROKEN* triptych of performance pieces. Like *Jesus* (in which I carried a cross the thousand miles from Moncton to Toronto and invited people at a gallery there to help nail me onto it) and *Thích Quảng Dúc* (in which I used gasoline and a spark from two rocks rapped together to set my clothes alight, and left onlookers to douse me), this work is designed to be *long* and *dangerous* and *painful* and *pointless*.

Long because only fatigue will render me incapable of acting, specifically of acting like a performance artist. I must be reduced to being myself, whatever that might turn out to be.

Dangerous because only the possibility of harm will force me to be present, which is the point of this and every other work of art. Any piece that isn't potentially fatal is dead.

Painful because pain is the body's way of registering danger. Pain is destructive, and what it destroys is whatever you were thinking a minute ago, whatever trick your mind was using to keep you lashed to the hands of the clock.

Pointless because any trace of narrative coherence will suck me and my audience back into time. A substantial stretch of uninflected anxiety will lead us through boredom to some other place.

The instructions for the piece are as follows:

- I stand naked and alone on a dais at one end of the gallery (TBA). My sole task is to remain conscious and upright for the duration of the piece, a maximum of twenty-four hours, if I live that long. Other than standing, I perform only unavoidable actions (urinating, weeping, etc.).

- A man-shaped, man-sized hourglass stands six feet away from me, a drawn bow in his arms. He is rigged such that he will loose his arrow once all the sand has passed through his radically-narrowed waist.

- The arrow is aimed at my heart.

- The man's waist, and thus the rate at which the sand flows, is flexible. At its initial setting, the hourglass will empty itself after approximately twelve hours. Any member of the audience may speed up or slow down time at any time, and thus shift the odds of my survival.

- If I survive one full day, the piece is complete. During that day I do everything in my power not to collapse. What collapses is the rigmarole of self which keeps me separate from my audience and them separate from me, and each of us separate from everything else in the universe.

In *The Lovers*, Marina Abramović (see her letter of support, attached) and her lover walked from opposite ends of the Great Wall of China and met in the middle to say goodbye. *Cupid* is my breakup with life, or my reunion with life, one or the other. It is dedicated to my on-again off-again partner Oji Gray (see his letter of support, attached), whose likeness (rocking his current look, mid FtM transition) will be tattooed onto my left breast, above my heart.

There will be no rehearsal and only one performance. When Marina was young she painted dreams and then car accidents and then clouds as they formed and dissolved. This is the truth. I will die if no one shows up, or if no one intervenes to retard time. I will live if I collapse, but I will not collapse. If I live it will be because the audience was moved by love and mercy rather than by something else. When Marina invited people to do whatever they wanted to her (in, for instance, *Rhythm 0*, for which she equipped them with various weapons and granted them absolute freedom), some savaged her but others succoured her. There is no way to know, and this is the point.

The point is that you're only your body, but your body isn't what you think it is.

I am applying for the maximum grant. As detailed in the attached budget, I require food and supplies for four months of training (at an abandoned trapper's cabin belonging to my uncle, near Moose Factory on James Bay). Like Marina I am subject to severe migraines, ideal preparation for this form of expression, but my suffering must of course be intensified in advance of each new piece.

The remainder of the budget is for the creation of an hourglass trans man, pudgy like a renaissance Cupid but with a waist like Oji's, which is to say with a waist like Scarlett O'Hara's once Mammy has done with her.

Pain and beauty. Beauty and pain.

Thank you for your time and consideration.

Voicemail

Emilia checked messages the minute they got in the door. A reflex, and an irksome one as far as Steve was concerned, especially since almost nobody called the landline anymore. What was she hoping for? What did she dread?

He tossed his jacket, rooted in the fridge for a beer. Bad enough to be at an art opening. Worse to be at your girlfriend's ex's art opening, and worse still to be at your girlfriend's ex's art opening and find there's no bar.

"This one's for you," said Emilia, and she replayed it on speaker. *Hi, it's Bridget. I'm calling for Steve. He knows why.* A few fitful breaths and then, *Toodle-oo.*

So, an evening of exes. What was weird was that he'd almost thought of Bridget earlier on. One of Patrick-the-prick's paintings was, if you could be objective for just a moment, kind of good. Steve had been trying to look absorbed in it so he'd be left alone, and suddenly found that he was absorbed. The painting was on plexiglass, and maybe wasn't a painting at all but some sort of messed-with collage. Realistic images had been bled into abstraction – it was cool because you didn't always know what you were looking at, or if you were looking at the right thing. The little card on the wall no doubt explained how the effect had been achieved, and offered a disambiguating title, but Steve's one policy at art galleries was never to look at those little cards. Should a man not let himself see what he sees?

Certain objects had survived. In the lower left-hand corner, a candlestick teetered on the edge of what appeared to be the gunwale of a canoe. At dead centre, an eye, likely that of a goat, gazed out of its mail-slot pupil. Steve gazed back. He unlistened to Emilia and the prick murmuring civilly to one another on the far side of the room – or more than civilly, they were laughing together now at something Patrick had just said – and to the animated chatter of various people he should but didn't know by name. He allowed his focus to trace an architectural projection of some kind up into the piece's pewter sky, and then east across a series of amber striations. In the top right corner, the plug of a fire hydrant curled cozily, orangely in on itself. If you saw this swirl as a cat it would be Bridget's tabby from back in the day, the one who'd station himself at the foot of her bed and growl whenever you got Bridget moaning. Steve didn't quite have this thought at the time, but saw now that he could have.

"So why?" said Emilia.

"What?"

"Bridget. She says you'll know why she called."

"Oh, I'm not sure. She was pretty sick at one point, maybe it's that. Farewell call, sort of thing."

Emilia was in the middle of slipping her bra out from under her blouse. She paused, bra hanging from her sleeve. "Like, she's *dying?* What of?"

"Breast cancer. I told you."

Had he? This was the worst thing about lying, or one of the worst, having to keep track. Steve never lied to Emilia about anything else, but about Bridget he couldn't stop. Right at the start, three years ago, he told her he and Bridget were finished, whereas in fact he was still succumbing to occasional regret-sex with her. He also claimed she'd left him, whereas in fact he'd left her. And now, for no good reason, here he was pretending not to have been following her on social media, tracing the ups and downs of her remissions and recurrences, even sending the odd supportive message and signing off *love as always S*. No good reason indeed – Emilia was almost insultingly unjealous, as though the thought of Steve straying, or for that matter finding somebody to stray with, was absurd. She seemed to trust him, too, perhaps because she knew he trusted her.

Emilia pulled her bra the rest of the way out of her sleeve. "I'm sorry," she said. "You did tell me." She touched Steve's shoulder.

"No worries," said Steve. "Some decent stuff tonight, hey? Of Patrick's?"

"Beautiful, his best ever." Emilia spun her bra like a lariat once or twice, then scrunched it up and stuffed it in her pocket.

Steve said, "I've been a bit of a dick to him, haven't I? I should have said something tonight."

"No, you were fine. Don't think about that. Think about … yikes. What will you say to her? Bridget, I mean."

"I don't know. What does a person say to somebody who's, you know, not going to be alive pretty soon?"

Emilia frowned. "A person? I think it's you we're talking about, Steve."

Mystifying, this thing with Bridget. People talked about the end of a relationship as a death, but surely it was the other way around. Surely what killed you was the start of a relationship. Once you were with one person you *were* one person, you were nobody else. You were born, so you'd die. So then Bridget, all the times he'd fantasized about her over these last few years, represented the possibility of a new life for him, a rebirth, a reincarnation. Which left him where, now that she was done for?

"Did she ever find somebody else?" said Emilia.

"Bridget? Yeah, I'm pretty sure."

It made the whole thing worse, Bridget still being single. It made his lying and fantasizing worse, and it made Bridget's predicament worse, no one to hear or hold her. She'd always been crazy for contact, spooning him at night, her small breasts flattened big against his back. Those breasts were gone now – she'd posted from the hospital after having them removed, linking to a piece about Angelina Jolie undergoing the same surgery. *She got to keep her nipples, the lucky biatch!!!*

Steve thought he might cry. "I gotta go call her," he said.

He took a last slug of his beer. "I'll do it from out on the steps so I don't bug you."

"Okay. But there's something we need to talk about."

"Yeah?"

"Later. Tomorrow. I'm sorry. Tell her I'm sorry, okay?"

"Sure," said Steve.

Sorry. Maybe that's what he should say too. Sorry I broke up with you. Sorry I haven't been any help since you got your news. Sorry I've used you, the ever-amenable you in my head, and offered nothing in exchange.

"Sorry," said Steve.

"No," said Emilia. "For what?"

"I need to be better."

"Don't say that," she said. "Please don't say that." And she really seemed to mean it.

About Me

I'm a fun-loving guy looking to be a little less alone for whatever time I have left. My friends, those who still have command of their senses, would describe me as aporetic, puzzled to the point of dismay. I like walks at sunset but rarely take them. Perhaps with you. I'm most deeply drawn to music that can be played by a string quartet on period instruments, but a colleague of mine once went through a bluegrass phase and I found myself humming "Bible in the Cabin by the Sea," so anything's possible. My favourite author is Chuang Tzu, a Taoist of the fourth century BC. I won't bore you with him or any of his aphorisms. I like bourbon, which is odd because I've never been anyplace where that's what you drink.

You'll notice I've left "Pets?" blank. My dog Dionysus died of kidney failure last week. Do I have a pet or don't I?

You'll notice I've left "Do you want children?" blank. I have four children, none of whom I understand, but all of whom I adore. They are shards of their shattered mother, whose decline is something from which I'll never mend. I want children, and I have them. If you have some that'll be great too.

You'll notice I've left "Age?" blank. As we all do, I forgot everything when I was born, unremembered the perfections I'd witnessed in the fleshless eternity between my little lives. Since, as Socrates argues, "all nature is akin" (συγγενοῦς), it was necessary for me to recall just one thing, and everything else began to come back. Now it's slipping away again. Age? I'm at that moment in life at which anamnesis, the recovery of forsaken insight, tips over into senility. I'm forgetting exactly as fast as I remember.

"Kum ba yah," for instance, the folksong my wife took to singing in her final months, when she could no longer speak. Sometimes I recall that the phrase means "come by here," other times I don't. I lose it, not just the literal meaning but the notion itself, that something supreme might inhere. I'm curious to see how long it will take this idea to desert me altogether. If there's a saviour it is this kind of curiosity.

What else? I don't have a favourite colour, though if I did I suppose it would be the red of a candy apple. My johnson still works now and again. I run, or rather ran, a moderately successful closet and garage storage solutions business. I'd like to hear some things about you.

You'll notice I've left "Do you do drugs?" blank. There wasn't enough room. Atenolol, Dabigitran, Ramipril, Flomax, Finasteride, Rosuvastatan, Synthroid, Lasix, Citalopram.

"If you hide the universe in the universe you can never be robbed of it." Sorry, I lied when I said I wouldn't bore you with any aphorisms. My friends, those who still have command of their senses, would say I rarely lie.

Am I signing up here in a fit of grief over Dionysus? Quite possibly, but I'm of the opinion that there's a deeper impulse, a truer one.

I seem to be having difficulty with the "She wants to meet up" feature. If you click on me and don't hear back, this may be the reason. I would ask you to try again.

Date

She spots him half a block away. One of the Mitchell boys, the
one who didn't die, obviously. Ricky. Ronny? He's on the far
side, maybe he won't cross over. It was Ronny who died. Or
Ricky? A few years after they all graduated, twenty-five years
ago now. Good lord. The story was he lost a bet he could hold
his breath under water for two minutes. Or won it, in a way –
he never came up. Ricky found him there under the dock, if
it was Ronny who died, or vice versa. They were twins, not
identical but the other kind. Both of them were chunky, and
had that ridiculous red hair. Ricky was the one who asked
her out a couple of times. She should have gone. It might have
saved her from Ken Grant, that conceited brute, which would
have saved her a nervous breakdown, which would saved her
all sorts of other troubles too. Who knows, maybe it would
also have sent Ricky off in some other direction, maybe he

wouldn't have had to die, if he was the one who did. *Fraternal.* Fraternal twins, which meant they were just plain old siblings, like her and Helen. If she died, or Helen died, would people remember which one? Would it matter? Like at dinner the other night, squabbling with Martin about whether it was Frank or Charles from *M*A*S*H* who died. Not squabbling, but yes, squabbling.

Yikes. He's glancing over her way, Ronny or Ricky. She slows, peers into a shop window. Kids' stuff, and she does need something for her friend Nicole's daughter's baby shower. The first grandchild in their group. It isn't fair, really, that she and Martin have just the one kid and he turns out to be gay. Of course she loves her son-in-law, Jamal, she couldn't have hoped for anybody better, unless he was a daughter-in-law instead. But there are lots of gay couples adopting, or maybe not lots but some. Or finding surrogates. Hopefully they'd use Bill's sperm, though to be honest Jamal is smarter and better looking, plus she might end up passing on the diabetes through Bill. It can skip a generation. That's probably what will carry her off, some organ that's given out because of the wonky sugar in her blood, though what carried her off in her dream last night was a salmon, one of those ones with the hooked jaw, which meant it was male. Or did that mean it was female? It struggled upstream with her and lost her in amongst the rocks, which were actually books, dictionaries of all sorts of other languages she used to know but had forgotten. Funny. In high school she took Spanish, and either Ricky or Ronny was in that class too, or maybe both. *Dónde está* something-or-other. Where's the loo?

Oh, dear. She catches his reflection in the shop window as he crosses the street. Yep, it's him, Ricky or Ronny. She busies herself trying to make out the price tag on a little kids' tent set up in the shop window. Maybe not the most sensible gift for somebody who hasn't yet been born, but –

"Helen?"

She turns. "Um, no."

"Oh, I'm sorry. From the side you just … I'm sorry." He's not as portly as you'd expect, after all these years. He's minus most of the ridiculous red hair.

"Helen's my sister."

"Yes, so you're … You won't remember me, but I'm Ricky's brother. I was in your year too."

"Of course." She smiles, steps forward. It never hurts to be pleasant to people. "I'm Val. I was … we were all so sorry to hear."

"Val," he says. "Thank you. It's a long time ago now."

"It is."

A brief silence. He opens his mouth, closes it, opens it again. "I actually … it's odd remembering this. I actually came along on that date."

"Date?"

"You and Ricky. His plan was to take you swimming, just the two of you, but he lost his nerve and wanted me along." Ronny shrugs. "I was the outgoing one, as you may recall."

"No."

"Anyway, it was a big deal for him. He almost never spoke to girls, but he was crazy about you."

"I'm afraid you're mistaken."

"No, you wouldn't have known, he wouldn't have made much out of it. But he was smitten."

"I'm saying you're mistaken about the date. Ricky asked me out, but I didn't go."

"Didn't go?"

"I was seeing Ken Grant. Remember, from rugby?" She finds herself making an absurd huggish sort of gesture, as though to lock Ronny in a scrum.

"But —"

"I *wish* I'd gone, believe me."

"Ah."

"Stupid girl."

"No. I mean, I certainly didn't mean …" Ronny looks about, apparently in search of a clue as to where he'd been headed.

She says, "I really do wish that."

"Thank you," he says. "Listen, you take care now, okay? And give my best to Helen, will you? I had a big crush on her." He chuckles in a self-deprecating way, turns and strides off.

She turns too, back to the shop window. A clerk is just climbing into the display to fetch a teddy bear, or actually a fuzzy baboon. The little red tent — fifty dollars, can that be right? Far too much for a make-believe tent. Imagine crawling in there, though, you and a brother or sister. How safe that would feel.

Earthlings

Apogee is different, since we lost Perigee. She yowls even more, and she keeps trying to throw up, to empty her empty stomach. She sleeps at Perigee's end of the padded cage, which I've moved into the crew capsule so she can be closer to me. She'll startle for no reason, and swim weightlessly around in tight little circles, a decaying orbit with the pull of a black hole at its centre. Is this what grief looks like, for a cat? Growing up, my sister and I were only ever allowed guinea pigs. We'd have a funeral each time one "joined the choir celestial," as Mum would say, and I'd marvel at what seemed even to me like the disproportionate depth of my despair. I failed to be curious about how its buddies felt. Incredible, how much of my life I've spent not noticing, or noticing only what was already evident to me.

It was Gabi, it was my colleague Dr. Gabisile Nkosi, who renamed the cats just before our launch. Apogee, the point in a terrestrial orbit that's furthest from the earth. Perigee, the point that's closest. Nerdy names, but also kind of perfect. "O-Apogee, O-Apogee," I sing, like "Awimbawe," the chanty background bit of "The Lion Sleeps Tonight." If Gabi were here she could do the other bit. She probably had a better singing voice than I do. It couldn't have been much worse.

Perigee died this morning (granted, time of day doesn't mean much when you circle the earth every ninety minutes), Gabi last night. Gabi was out trying to see where we'd been struck, what systems might be restored. We did rock paper scissors. I lost. Our mission had already been aborted, it was a matter of mustering enough control for a re-entry. The chances of Gabi being hit too were minuscule. We must have passed through a cloud of debris, a busted up old satellite or some such. At seventeen thousand miles an hour, a fleck of metal will barely slow as it drills through you.

Our whole lives we're bullied by gravity. We obey, we knuckle under. The longing to get free, isn't that just gravity talking too? This is the kind of thought I'd share with Petra, if I had one more chance.

Apogee paddles her way over to nuzzle my fingers when I poke them through the bars of her cage. She doesn't seem to have any desire to get buckled back into what Gabi called her "blastoff box," and I'm not going to insist. I've unplugged her from the hard drive that was capturing her data – the hookup on her head looks like a tiny little top hat. She's lucky we missed our rendezvous, or at least this is the story I'm telling her. She's better off to orbit with me for a few more hours and then die (I'll have to devise a way to kill her when the time comes, when our life support begins to shut down for good) than to be gradually dismantled on the space station. With no weight to bear she'd have declined like a little old lady, muscles atrophying, bones growing porous, and the team would have done whatever it took to extract information that might one day be useful to us. Like every other thing, animate or inanimate, she'd have been transformed into a text for us to read, a reservoir of data for us to drain. I keep apologizing to her for that, and for everything else. This, where we are right now – whistling pointlessly around the planet, a couple of carbon-based creatures wedged into a boy's toy – this is where we've been headed all along. I knew it, but she did not.

I say a couple of carbon-based creatures, but in fact there are a whole lot of us. A veritable Noah's ark, this ship, though heavy on "lower" life forms – the folks in back are all insects and amphibians. Of what suffering might they be capable? Is it possible that they're grieving too, as their kin perish? How would I know? I gaze godlike down from space, taking note of how clueless I am about myself and my fellow earthlings.

As a kid, I loved cheetahs, for their speed. My sister Soph loved lions, for their strength. Oh God, my sister Soph. They'll have brought her in by now, on the chance that we might regain communication. And Petra, though our relationship is almost too new to count. And of course Gabi's people, her husband and two daughters, since as far as they know she's still in here with me, not mummified and towed behind us on her tether. *Horizon, this is Mission Control Houston. Do you read?*

Sometime out in the middle of our last night together – we were soaking in the bathtub, thoroughly soused on one another – Petra got serious. She asked me if I ever have doubts about the way I've chosen to spend my time, if I ever regret letting myself be "seduced by velocity" – she meant my flying career, I think, but also the way I've confessed to careening through my private life. Could I imagine another route to transcendence, another way out of whatever it is we're all stuck in? Her voice was wistful, and so soft she might have meant it as more pillow talk. Looking back, I realize she was trying to tell me something about herself, about the grim frenzy of her own past. I should have asked her, but instead I answered. I hope she's forgotten whatever I said by way of evasion.

Both of us have been lost a long time. Do we not deserve a little found time together? Then again, getting what you deserve, is that the point of this particular universe?

Apogee's on the move again, bunting herself about the cage like a calico balloon. I've explained to her that it's an illusion, this experience of weightlessness. I've explained that we aren't actually drifting but dropping, in free fall around the earth. For now, the pull of the planet is perfectly offset by our forward momentum. It's like jumping out a too-high window, I tell her. Until you land, it's liberty.

She isn't much interested in this kind of talk. She likes it better when I sing.

Skywalker

Amongst the papers my mother left behind when she died —
files from old court cases, mostly, the failed prosecutions
by which she was most vividly haunted — was the draft of a
mystery novel. Under its title, *Song of the Skull*, she'd supplied
a couple of highbrow epigraphs, pulled, presumably, from the
fat volumes of philosophy she kept on her bookshelf. I'd never
seen her open one, but then again I seem to have missed a
lot. Spinoza: "Each thing, as far as it can by its own power,
strives to persevere in its being." And Heraclitus: "Everything
flows, nothing remains." What we want is to keep being what
we are, or imagine ourselves to be. What we want is exactly
what we can't have.

Mother had concocted a challenging pair of murders.
First to die was a young Indigenous activist seeking to have
certain human remains repatriated to the people of the land
from which they'd been stolen a century earlier. Suspicion

for the murder was directed at the curator of the museum, who was disturbingly zealous in his efforts to prevent those remains being released. He acknowledged that it was wrong to exhibit the bones of First Nations people, but couldn't grasp the necessity of returning them. His shaky rationale in this particular case was that Luke (as he'd taken to calling the collection of bones labeled L640) had been dead seven thousand years, and might not be related to anybody who now lived in the area. The only way to confirm this, or refute it, would be to perform further DNA and other tests on Luke's skeleton, precisely the kind of desecration from which the band was seeking to spare him.

But then the curator was killed too. He had his throat slit with a Neolithic flint blade, of the sort Luke himself would have wielded, filched from the museum's collection. This was the same fate that had befallen the activist. Same M.O., so same attacker? Who would want both of them dead? Who stood to gain from silencing both sides?

There were other twists too. Most of the books on Mother's shelves were mysteries, and she knew her stuff, knew what it took to entice and befuddle a reader. Might the whole thing have been a hoax, the bones planted by somebody out to make mischief? Might the first murder have been a hate crime (there'd been a rash of such killings in the community a couple of years earlier), the second an attempt to cover it up? And so on, a whole host of obfuscating prejudices and desires.

Mother's taste was for hardboiled American mysteries, but she looked more the part of an Agatha Christie character – the slightly addled aunt, say, who notices things she oughtn't.

Her style on the page was a curious hybrid of the two, the gritty and the effete. She'd had a go at adding colour to her story through evocations of Indigenous life, about which she knew nothing. This was painfully obvious, even to another outsider like me, but the earnest generosity of her imaginings went some way to make up for it. She'd risked a few fancy moves, for instance granting the activist a vision in which she fought and found herself bayoneted by a white man on the field of an old battle. She remained conscious, indeed serene, as her skull was measured and found to be "primitive," supposed proof that she and her people were inferior to the invaders who were engineering their extinction. The vision ended – I've never admired Mother more – with a glimpse of the white man, older now, a raving syphilitic, face caved in like a rotten gourd, baying at a lantern he'd mistaken for the moon.

Mother's mystery worked, in the sense that it made me crave a solution. Fortunately I'd skipped ahead (I've never been able to bear suspense) to find that there wasn't one. Mother had left her book unfinished. I've searched her records, rummaged through her files, digital and otherwise, and found no evidence that she knew who to hold responsible for the two deaths. Her weakness as a lawyer – a weakness I've inherited, along with the profession – was a tendency to be overwhelmed by conflicting narratives. Perhaps this flaw stymied her as an author as well, made it impossible for her to home in on one culprit. Or perhaps she simply ran out of time. Her death was sudden, as sudden as an assault she might have visited upon one of her characters.

It's the other mystery that most matters to me, of course. Why did Mother keep her mystery novel to herself? In a way, it's no mystery at all. She and I were never intimate, not since I was a boy. When Mother and I talked, we talked about work, about nuances of the law that seemed to escape our colleagues. Intimacy of a sort, but we steered clear of the more personal confidences that tend to signify a family bond. Mother would once in a while hint that it was time I put down roots, found somebody special, but she did so in a way that made the notion sound even more farfetched than I already believed it to be. The most confessional she'd get on her own account would be to muse, now and then, about trying a whodunit for herself. It disheartened her that she hadn't any ideas. Despite a career spent prosecuting criminals, she was stumped when it came to devising a crime of her own. What ultimately clicked for her? And what made her feel the need to conceal her inspiration from me?

It was a matter of delicacy, as best I can piece it together. Respect for the dead. To explain the Indigenous theme to me, Mother would have had to reveal that she herself was Indigenous, or partly so. To explain that, she would have had to reveal that her father wasn't her father, that her mother went AWOL for a few months at the start of their marriage, fleeing her new husband for the charms of a guy named Randy Rice. All of this, or most of it, was discovered by a distant cousin of Mother's who'd retired and taken to puttering at genealogy. Mother learned of her complicated parentage a couple of years before she died, but kept the knowledge to herself. She clearly used it to try to make sense of the disturbances in her own upbringing, and thus in mine. She took to brooding in private about the ongoing injustices visited upon a people with whom she now felt so connected. Since she didn't have it in her to rant, she sought to encode her outrage in a mystery story. That story, the process of crafting it, seems to have intensified her feelings to the point that they couldn't be expressed.

Randy Rice was Mohawk. He would have said that he was of the *Kanien'kehá:ka*, the People of the Flint Nation. Or at least I believe that's what he'd have said — my ignorance is, to be truthful, largely intact. He appears to have been a "sky-walker" (thus the cute "Luke" clue from Mother, a nod to my childhood obsession with *Star Wars*), one of the many men of his people who worked the high steel. I haven't been able to determine if he was ever in New York City, but it's on the Empire State Building that I imagine him, guiding a girder into place a thousand feet above the teeming city. Ladies in cloche hats, men in fedoras.

I picture him, my grandfather, or I try to. Envision him. My grandfather, his father, his father's father, and so on. I turn around and go the other way, forward in time but by a different route — I picture me if my settler forebears hadn't fled their own lives, if they'd never overrun this land and leached into my bloodstream. I picture me at home here. I picture me at home anywhere, a stranger to nothing.

Savasana

Ed drives, Mel fiddles with the radio. Her parents' place is far enough out of town that they lose the public radio station and have to find it again on a different frequency, which they can never remember one visit to the next. Ed had been half listening as another aria was introduced. Something from *Rigoletto*, which he's pretty sure he hates, though hating is something on which he's been trying to cut back. "Gilda," said the guy on the radio, "is happy to die for her lover, the cad. Better perhaps to say she dies for love ..."

"If my father offers you a second glass," says Melanie, "you say no."

"I do, do I?"

"You do. Please."

"Even though he'll go ahead and have a second glass himself. And a third, and a fourth, and start explaining to me how he saw the whole thing coming."

"What whole thing?"

"Exactly."

Mel continues to poke at buttons, getting blurts of news, weather, wimpy rock 'n' roll. "Besides, with your pills."

Ed lowers his window, lets the evening air lash at his face. "You know that thing where if you die in a dream you die for real?"

"If he pours a fourth, we leave," says Melanie. "That's a myth."

"You think so? Have you ever died in one?"

"I'm not sure. Yes, once, definitely." She gets *Rigoletto*, cranks it up to cover the roar of the wind, but it's too staticky. She shuts it off. "Guess we're in between."

"Because actually, how could you dream you're dead? Who'd dream it?"

"I drowned, and I washed up on the rocks, and the sun dried me and then I was okay. I was alive." She shrugs, bewildered, and then worried. "Why, have you been having bad sleeps again? I heard you up last night."

"Mm, odd sleeps." The road curves closer to the shore, Ed accelerating to intensify the tug on his body. Bits of sunset bounce off the waves at them through a thin fence of fir trees.

"Maybe I should drive," she says. "Want me to drive?"

"I keep waking up. I go to touch Galia, and before I can reach her, I'm awake."

"Galia."

This isn't fair, sharing this. But would it be fair to shut it up inside? What he's supposed to be doing is getting things out in the open, releasing the pressure.

She says, "Like, *Galia?*"

"Yeah. She's in the camel pose. Or sometimes the cobra. *Bhujangasana.*"

"I know the names, Ed."

His favourite is the corpse pose, *savasana.* You lie there, is what you do. *Give up your body*, murmurs Galia. *Give up your mind.* He's come close, a time or two. The peace, the permeable sense of self Mel and the others seem to experience – he's almost made contact. And then, maddeningly, felt himself recoil.

"Why are you trying to touch her?" says Mel. "And I mean, *where* are you trying to touch her?"

"Just ... anywhere." It was Mel's idea, him signing up. Beginners' class, a new way to work on his troubles. Purer, more positive. "That's not the point."

"Okay. What's the point?" She turns his way. "It's weird, right? We barely touch for months, and then you dream about touching another woman and –"

"*Trying* to touch another woman. I reach out, but then I wake up, every time."

"Every time? Like, how many times?"

"I don't know, Mel. Does that matter? The point is, it's like falling, and then just before you hit ... boom. You're awake."

"So ...?"

"So maybe you didn't drown. You were under water, but still breathing."

Mel sighs, slumps back.

Ed steers hard into another curve, lets the last of the sun come at him. "For a little while, you can do that."

191

Frantic

My ex-boyfriend's favourite book was *Dead Souls*. Sounds dead serious, but I've read it and it's actually funnier than you think, kind of like him, like Mike. This guy's going around Russia buying up dead souls, meaning dead serfs who still exist on paper. It's eighteen something-or-other. I already forget what he plans to do with them, but it's hilarious and also smart because he's dead too, the guy is, like living dead, corrupt and empty and everything. I wish I'd read it last year, when I was still going out with Mike. It might have helped.

At first you thought Mike was serious, then you realized he was funny, then you realized he was serious. What got him about Gogol, the guy who wrote *Dead Souls* (I used to say it google, just to bug Mike, but it's actually goggle), was he wanted to be taken seriously, but everybody just thought he was funny. He had these big religious ideas about his book, even though it was a riot. So he started writing a part two, where the soul-buying-up guy gets enlightened. He gets a soul, basically, but Gogol had a hard time with it, part of which was that he realized he had to get himself a soul first, so he started to pray and not eat, which kind of messed with his writing. Plus he had this priest telling him his stuff was satanic, which didn't help either. Eventually Gogol burned part two, so he wouldn't go to hell, and starved himself to death.

Reading it probably wouldn't have helped, but who knows. I'd still have had to break up with Mike, but he might have thought better of me afterwards. I might have thought better of myself. How can you not read the favourite book of some-body you're so into? How spineless do you have to be? Mike didn't read my favourite book either (I never told him my favourite book, I was too embarrassed), but he watched my favourite movie, and listened to my favourite band. He told me the lead singer of Formerly Known As Formerly Known As Frantic was gay, which maybe should have been a clue. Mike was always telling you who was gay, politicians and profs and everything (he was already in first year, which was part of the turn-on for miss goody-two-shoes here). Mike's theory was that Gogol was gay, that was the real reason he starved himself. So then Mike started starving himself too, which suited him, those cheekbones. Dead smart, and dead beauti-ful. Which makes you think, what was he doing with me in the first place? And who really broke up with who? When you keep catching your boyfriend staring at your Frantic poster, and everybody in Frantic's a guy, are you really the one who called it off?

Also, where's Gogol now? Can you save yourself by killing yourself? Mike didn't think so, so he stopped not eating and let himself fall in love with one of his profs. That didn't work (Mike isn't all that good at knowing who's gay, it turns out), but it got him going. Whereas I'm in first year now, and I'm totally stuck. I have no issue, no problem. I'm not gay or anorexic or anything, I'm just alone, and that's a lame reason for feeling like this. I've cut myself a few times, but who hasn't? I started to carve "Mike" into my arm one time, but I only got as far as "M." I've been trying to think, what else does that stand for? What else could I say?

Canoe Lake

Sal says I was dead for a bit there – I passed out in the men's room at Panic, end of a decent night of partying, and she had to come get me – but she's wrong. I know she's wrong because what I had wasn't a near-death experience. I didn't feel peace and contentment. I didn't hear a whooshing sound. I didn't enter a dark tunnel, and I didn't look back down on my body as it went cold. Nana wasn't there to greet me, and neither was Weeze and neither was Spongebill, neither were any of the people I've known well enough to be messed up now that they're gone. My past didn't flash in front of me like the trailer for some sorry-assed film, thank Christ.

Pretty much the only thing that fit was the Being of Light, and even that, she wasn't light so much as pale, the goth sort of pale that's sexy on a certain kind of woman. But on Ms. Wadzinski from elementary school? And it wasn't love and acceptance coming off her, at least not at first. Disappointment? Something like that but stronger, stranger.

I was supposed to do Tom Thomson – this is in real life, this is what happened to me back in grade six – his art and also his thing with the Group of Seven and the mystery of his death by drowning in Algonquin Park. Was there foul play involved? What were his artistic influences? All that.

So I did him, but half-assed. Wad was counting on me, and I let her down. I had like one piece of Bristol board with a copy of a painting in the middle, a rocky point with a pine tree crippled over in the wind. I had a photograph of Tom Thomson and his canoe, and a map with an x marking the spot on Canoe Lake where his body was found corking around with a ding in the skull, and a couple of paragraphs of bio copied onto a sheet of foolscap. "Accident? Murder? Suicide? We may never know." Pathetic. The kind of thing Cody Scott might have handed in, but from Cody it would have been okay because that's what he was capable of. Wad knew that, so she wouldn't have been sad, whereas when I handed in my effort I honestly thought she was going to cry. One crappy project and I broke her heart.

So there she was in my vision or whatever – this is last Friday when I passed out at Panic and didn't die – pale and pretty and for some reason sitting on the high windowsill in the boys' room down in the basement of the old school, which is gone now, in real life, just an empty lot. Sun was coming from behind her so I suppose you could see that as angelic, but the setting pushed it the other way, the pee-stink from the trough mixed with the bleachy smell of the janitor's mop. Juvenile hell.

Wad was still grieving, there in my head. She was dead and everything (she died for real when I was in high school, which freaked us out because she was so young and almost hot), but what was still destroying her after twenty years was my Tom Thomson project. "How could you refuse that opportunity?" she wanted to know. "Tom Thomson, and you with such an eye for colour. You really were good, you know."

"Me?" I said. "Good?"

She ran a hand through her hair, which was seaweed. "It would be one thing if I'd assigned you the parliamentary system, or the water cycle, or even beavers. But Tom Thomson? Why would you settle for such a perfunctory job?"

You could take that as a sign, I suppose. *Perfunctory* is a word I know, but just barely, and I could go a billion years without using it. So maybe it really was Wad talking, and not just my fainted-guy fantasy of her. Maybe she really came to me.

I had no answer to the perfunctory thing, the question of why I'd failed her, so she moved on. She talked about Tom Thomson's crazy way of seeing the world and what might have granted him that vision. "He must have been on something, I suppose," she said. "No way a person could just be inspired, right? Bud, do you figure? Shrooms? Goofballs? Special K?"

"Lay off," I said. She was trying to make me feel like garbage, and it was working.

"Oxy? Mesc? Horse? Rock? Robo?"

"Robo?" I said. "You've got me chugging cough medicine? That's your opinion of me? I've never done that, I've never done most of that crap." Which was true, as long as you took "never" to mean "not for a while."

Wad grimaced, the way she'd grimace at Cody or some kid like that before she handed out a detention. "Xylophone," she said.

"Z-y –"

"Incorrect."

"I was messing with you. X-y."

Wad exhaled. "Was his painting musical, would you say? Tom Thomson's? He came from a family of musicians."

Which is another weird one, because there actually were musicians in Tom Thomson's family, but I didn't know that till I looked it up after the night at Panic. So maybe that's another sign that she really was a spirit or whatever, not just a blip in my head. Or maybe it was just a fluke, a detail my imagination made up that happened to be true. How would you know? How would you ever know anything?

"I find Tom Thomson's paintings intensely musical," I said. "Rhythmic. Harmonic."

Wad shook her head, unconvinced. She invited me to look at the pine tree painting again – she'd somehow got my Bristol board with her up on the bathroom's windowsill by this time. "Look carefully," she said, and I did. There was something about it, no question. "Are you in this painting?" she said. "Are you the wavy lake? Are you the rocky point? Are you the bendy tree?"

"I'm all of them," I said, just a wild guess, and she laughed as though we both knew this couldn't be true. She was busty just like I remember her, and wearing one of those tight sweaters, and after a while two circles of wet formed around her nipples, pasties of milk. If I told this part to Sal she'd say it was a rebirth symbol and it proved I was dead, so I'm not going to tell her. She keeps looking at me to see how I'm different since that day, and I'd like her to stop.

Wad kept on laughing even though I wasn't saying anything else funny. Her laugh started out cool but got warmer and warmer till it really did start to feel like love or something, and at a certain point it turned into my name. Then Sal was bending over me, there in the bathroom at Panic, not shaking me but calling my name right into my face. Her breath was like cloves, or at least I think that's what cloves smell like, and I had a hard-on which I hadn't had for a long time.

The thing is, I'd popped maybe forty mill of oxy that night with a couple of beers. Does Sal really think that would kill me? I could have had that tonight and no one would know. Actually, I have had that tonight. Also, if I was the one dying and Wad was there waiting for me, shouldn't it have been me asking the questions? Like what do you mean musical? What do you mean good?

Shrub

Most times, when Ron's father was about to die, Ron and Cate would both go. They'd take sick days, throw a couple of bags in the old Subaru and embark on the five-hour ferry-and-high-way trip to Ron's home town. There, by the metal-barred bed at Arbutus Manor, they'd commence their vigil. Within hours, a day or two at most, Ron's father would rally. His vital signs would stabilize. He'd regain a sort of breathy simulacrum of speech, and would ask, with admirable courtesy and composure, as he retrieved his hand from Ron's, who his two visitors might be. They'd pass an uncanny hour or so with him, then start the trip home, or, if it was too late, spend another night at the Ramada or the Travelodge or the Best Western. On the road they'd talk about what they should wish for. Was it okay to wish for somebody to die, when it was clear the life ahead would be increasingly impoverished and painful? Was there any way to be sure what portion of this wish was for the sake of the other person, and what portion was for you?

But this time Ron drew the line. Cate had been saddled with an extra course this term, and now her neck was acting up. No need for them both to endure the stress yet again. Cate protested, but in the end acquiesced.

So it was that Ron found himself solo on the ferry for the first time in many years. He treated himself to a few rounds in the dollar-a-shot massage chair – not something he'd do if Cate were along, though she'd probably get a kick out of it – and blew his heart-smart diet with the Big Man's Breakfast in the cafeteria. Outside on the upper deck he sipped coffee from a paper cup, let the wind whap his hair around. Gulls hovered like angels, like drones. Sheltering it with his body, he read through the little stack of pages he'd printed off before he set out. He'd found the material online a week or so ago, in the course of a panicky search for scraps of wisdom about death and how to deal with it. Back in the day, Cate had hauled around a copy of *The Tibetan Book of the Dead* – Ron could still call to mind its cover, a gaudy mandala grasped by a sharp-toothed deity. What he'd printed off this morning was a spoofy new angle on that book. Ron liked it. Whimsical as it was – perhaps precisely because of its whimsy – he believed it possessed the power to change him, to benignly mess with his notion of what it was to be him in the first place. He believed it had already done so.

O nobly born (insert name), let not thy mind be distracted.

This would have been lifted directly from the Tibetan original, making the text a pastiche, Ron supposed. A playful

takeoff. The idea was to recite it out loud to the dying person
to help him or her let go.

> O nobly born, that which is called death being come to
> thee now, picture this. You're in a futuristic gismo, kind
> of like that one in *Sleeper*, the Woody Allen movie, except
> instead of giving you an instant, effortless orgasm it tele-
> ports you to someplace else. Warsaw, say, unless that's
> where you already are.

Ron's father wouldn't get the Woody Allen reference. Would
he get any of it? Would he pick out the word "Warsaw," which
(Ron couldn't resist the tickle of this coincidence) happened
to be Ron's father's mother's birthplace? Probably not. Still,
it would be better than silence. Better to be reading out loud
than to be stuck listening in on the rude anarchy of his father's respiration. And who knew, some trace of the meaning
might thread its way through.

> The gismo scans you, and replicates you in Warsaw. A
> perfect copy, down to the atom, the electron, the quark.
> There are two you's now, but only for a short time, because
> the old you has been fatally damaged in the course of the
> replication. The old you lives just long enough to see the
> new you onscreen, and maybe compare a thought or two.
> "Are you me?" you say to the new you, and the new you
> nods. The new you believes he or she is you, which is what
> being you means. When you die, you don't die. There's
> nothing tragic here, nothing that needs to be clung to.

People had gathered at the ferry's railing. A woman gestured out to sea; phones were trained on some photo-worthy apparition. Orcas? Porpoises? Amazing what lived and died right here, within one's ken.

O nobly born, now imagine there's a glitch in the gismo. The eyes of the new you are slightly paler than yours. At first you think it's just the light in Warsaw at whatever time of day it is there, but no, the eyes are wrong. The new you isn't you, not exactly. Is this tragic?

Ron tried to picture himself at Arbutus Manor, actually reading this stuff out loud to his dad. Actually sharing it. If the old man were even marginally conscious it would take all Ron's courage. He couldn't possibly have done it back when his dad remembered who he was, and was still able to produce a cool, disparaging silence. He couldn't do it even today if Cate were there in the room with him. Strange. He'd always been like this, without ever quite noticing it before — he'd always carried on as though there were some vulnerable bit of him that needed to be cloistered, closed off.

Now imagine the error is a more significant one. The new you has darker hair. The new you responds, when you risk a little joke, with a laugh that's definitely goofier than yours. Is this tragic? The new you can name three more kinds of berry than you can name. The new you forgets the lyrics and resorts to humming along to "Who'll Stop the Rain," whereas you can sing it right through to the end.

Ron started to skim here – a recorded voice had announced that they were nearing the terminal. Over the course of a few paragraphs, the dying person was invited to envision a replication process that was more and more fundamentally flawed. The new person was less and less like the old one. Was there any particular stage at which the alteration became grievous? Was there any particular stage at which death became something that mattered? The tempo of the text gradually picked up, crescendo-ing. In the end the new person wasn't a person at all.

> The new you is a leopard. The new you is a seagull. The new you is a shrub.

It was at this point, on his first reading, that Ron finally got it, finally felt it all the way down. Here on the boat, the impact proved less potent. Perhaps it was the rush. Perhaps it was that he no longer felt needy enough. Perhaps you only got the full effect in a moment of desperation.

People were starting for the stairs – the ferry slowed for its contact with the dock. Ron folded up his papers and stuffed them away.

It was a sublime day for a drive. Lightly overcast, hardly another soul on the road, coniferous forest flashing inexhaustibly by on either side. Ron rolled down his window and cranked up his tunes, louder than he'd normally allow himself. Coleman Hawkins, Lester Young, a shuffle of all the great sax players he'd first encountered in his father's collection.

O nobly born Benjamin. Maybe if he boiled the thing down. What was the key, the kernel? What simple incantation might crack open the shell of his dad, incite in him the same inexplicable lightness, the same sense of liberation that Ron himself had experienced, however briefly?

Shrub. That was the word that had done it for Ron. *Shrub.* And there it was again, a flicker of the feeling. *Shrub.* Just a flicker, which Ron endeavoured not to lose even as the breath left him and the car swerved out of control. The thing was to submit. The thing was to surrender to the hard fact of the hand on his chest, the great hand that held him now and squeezed.

Stage

Oscar's just had his after-dinner dump so I'm juggling his leash and the loaded plastic bag when my cell phone rings, no chance to screen the call.

"Hello, my name's Annika. I'm calling from the Diabetes Association. How are you this evening, sir?"

It's tricky to isolate any one thought from the torrent of dreck that is my inner life, but I somehow latch onto the notion that I've got diabetes, and that this pleasant lady has rung me up to tell me so. It happens that I've been peeing a lot of late, plus there's Auntie Kay who's diabetic, the bad kind. There ought to be a whole other grief stage, call it Diagnosis, which is that you believe everything is wrong with you and with everybody you've ever loved. Since Jerry died I've had ulcers and bone cancer. Dad's had lupus. Butcher Bob's had emphysema.

Not that there even are stages of grief anymore, but Jerry drummed them into me back when Doctor Deb was helping him get over his mum. Now that I'm seeing Doctor Deb about Jerry she says it was all bull. "We fell in love with the stages," she says. "How they neatened everything up. Grief was something you chugged through, chug chug chug. The stages were ... the stages were a stage. But we've learned a lot since 9/11. There's no right way to grieve." I said to her last time, "So there are only wrong ways?" and she laughed, convinced that this was a good sign, my sense of humour coming back. For a shrink, she's really very poor at reading people.

"Sir?"

What's infuriating is that I'm the one who's always loved stages and steps and so forth. Jerry hated them, any attempt to box him up, move him out of exactly where he was at that exact moment. Six times I proposed to him before he'd even talk to me about marriage. When he finally said yes it was only because that was more random and ridiculous than saying no again. He still gave himself hell, though, for not following the stages over his mum, for being angry when he should have been in denial, for bargaining when he should have been depressed. And for feeling good, almost giddy, when that's no stage at all.

I kind of get it now, the feeling good bit. Jerry's only been gone three months and just yesterday I had a decent time with Oscar at Good Dawg, where I've been taking him for sessions once a week since he started acting out. There's another guy, Niklaus, who's got a schnoodle named Socrates,

and not romantically or anything but we've connected. I half
had Niklaus in mind when I masturbated last night. Wanking,
would that come before Anger or after it? Niklaus keeps
asking me how I'm *doing,* the emphasis to let me know he
really wants to know, but does he?

"Sir?"

Annika doesn't want to know, I'm confident of that.
Maybe I should tell her anyway. Back when there were stages
you talked about it all the time. Jerry was forever rattling
on about his mum, just exactly when her heart began to fall
behind, what he wished he'd said to her. In those days your
sadness was a foreign body you had to expel or it would fester,
and what if that's still true? *My gay husband died and I'm
alone* – I could jump right in. Never just husband, always
gay husband. Jerry's joke and I've kept it going, immortality and so on. *My gay husband died and I'm alone*, just
stark like that. Or I could go into a little more detail. *My
gay husband died of an aneurysm eighty-seven days ago at
a performance of a piece he wrote called "Nowhere," which
was basically a recording of him playing Haydn's* Seven Last
Words of Christ *on the kazoo, piped in through forty-two
speakers wrapped all around you, which adjusted digitally
to where you were as you moved around on this big blacked-
out stage so it always came evenly from everywhere, which
meant you were nowhere. You were always nowhere. It was
a concert for one so he died alone,* which wouldn't be true,
his sister was there with him, but sometimes the truth isn't
what happened.

"Um, sir?"

But now it's bad for you, getting it out. So says Doctor Deb. What you're doing is digging yourself deeper and deeper into the rut of your own horror. I already went over the story once today anyway, with Butcher Bob. He knows it well enough. Knows to laugh at *gay husband,* go quiet at *love of my life.*

"Hello, sir?"

And really, how can I be so sure? Was Jerry the love of my life? Am I dead yet? Do I want to be?

"Sir? I'm calling because you and your wife have supported us in the past."

I say, "My gay husband." Oscar's tugging at his leash — he keeps forgetting there's nobody at home. Perfectly natural, say the folks at Good Dawg, and he'll get over it, or at least he'll look as though he has, and what's the difference?

"Sir? Would there be a better time for me to call?"

"Yes," I say. "No," I say. "You know what? Now's good."

Many Worlds

It's the woman in the floral blouse, the older guy in the jean jacket, the Frida Kahlo look-alike, then you. Grab a *Newsweek* from the pile on the coffee table and pretend to pore over it. How lipstick saved lives at Bergen-Belsen. Climate change passes point of no return. Keep looking at the magazine but think about something else. Think about how hard it is not to think about something you don't want to think about. Think about the bizarre song you heard on the way over, Pink Floyd but with the Bee Gees in there too, somehow. Strange. Remember back to when strange was good. Remember back to when strange was fun because normal was always there when you needed it.

The woman in the floral blouse is up – the nurse, or maybe she's a receptionist, is guiding her into the doctor's office. Now it's just the older guy in the jean jacket, the Frida Kahlo look-alike, then you. Frida Kahlo in her mid-thirties, about the time of that self-portrait with the third eye that turns out to be a skull. Or a little later, the self-portrait as a deer shot full of arrows – Frida Kahlo at your age. Think positive, or rather think negative since that's what you need to hear, is negative. Is there something you can still do, some prayer or incantation that might still change the outcome of a test that's already been completed? The world is odd, remember. World, or worlds. Remember your physics. Remember you don't have any physics, but remember shooting the shit with the physics guys in the grad lounge, Sylas and Anoop. You quoting your Kierkegaard, them scribbling their math on beery napkins. "It is a lingering death, to be trampled to death by geese." Is this really the best bit of Kierkegaard you can conjure up? The point was that the equations only worked if there was more than one world, in fact if there were all possible worlds, if everything that can happen does happen. There's a world in which you remember a better bit of Kierkegaard. There's a world in which you remember that pithy bit about the absurd as the object of faith, in fact there's a world in which you not only remember that bit but recite it to the howled approval of the others here in the waiting room, including the receptionist who in many worlds has hair the colour of a smoggy sunset.

There goes the older guy in the jean jacket. Now it's just the Frida Kahlo look-alike, then you. She shrug-grimaces at you. Shrug-grimace back. Remember that in most worlds you don't exist, never have. Remember that in many of the worlds in which you do exist Allyson's here with you, since you didn't leave her just before your first symptom, if that's what that spell of weakness was. In countless worlds you met the Frida

Kahlo look-alike at a previous appointment, and went out afterwards for Mexican food – your clever idea – though she turned out to be Chilean. In some of those worlds you were suave yet authentic, yourself but somehow more than yourself, and the Frida Kahlo look-alike, long dark hair loosed from its braid, smiled as Frida Kahlo never did in any of her paintings, smiled as though the grief in her had been transformed into exaltation.

Hm. Some sort of mix-up here – the receptionist has called you first, ahead of the Frida Kahlo look-alike. Fine. Stroll, or better yet stride across the waiting room. En route, catch the eye of the Frida Kahlo look-alike. Determine to ask her her name when you come out. Paula? Sofia? Valentina? She bears all these names, and all others. All possibilities are realities, the thinkable ones and the unthinkable.

Creatures

Is it messed up to want my son to be the reincarnation of a man instead of a woman? Or small-minded or homophobic or something. It's too soon to say for sure whether or not he's gay, but the signs point the other way. I caught him Googling "big boobs" on my phone last weekend (though how big can they really be on that puny screen?), and his pajamas were crusty next morning. I called his mum with the news and she had a little cry over it, her baby no longer a boy. Then she said I could keep him for an extra couple of hours if I wanted to, and I said thanks, that would mean a lot. It's as though we forgot how to fight for a bit there, me and Philomena.

I love Max for who he is and everything, and of course I don't care if he's queer, but the animal thing is odd. Philomena hates animals, and not that it really matters but I do too. Us both not wanting pets was one of the things that made us imagine we could live together. When Max isn't around

217

I put food down for his cat Elsie, and I scoop her litter box, but I make sure she knows I bought and spayed her only to impress Max (about a week after I moved out of the house and into this dinky apartment), and that if not for him she'd be back on the street.

Elsie was my idea, actually. The name "Elsie." I thought it was funny, a cow's name for a cat, certainly better than the froufrou names Max kept coming up with, like "Sheba" and "Scheherazade." Then he saw *Born Free* at school one day (they were doing Africa in socials, with a teacher old enough to think that's what you show), and the lioness's name is Elsa. Elsie, Elsa. Philomena got hold of that coincidence, and combined it with Max's lifelong devotion to bugs and snakes and so on, and the whole reincarnation business just started rolling. Phil's a believer. She did a past life regression once that said she was a witch back when witches were being burned. For a while there, when things were extra bad between us, she fingered me for one of the priests who interrogated and tortured and roasted her alive for the sin of healing people. That was a rough patch. Anyhow, Max kept whistling the theme song from *Born Free* (which actually is kind of catchy), and getting more and more obsessed with nature, and Phil "put two and two together," as she says.

There are some pretty cool bits of evidence, if you were looking to be convinced. Max has these two blade-like birthmarks on his chest, and apparently Joy Adamson, the woman who raised Elsa and then let her back into the wild, was stabbed to death by an angry employee. Joy was almost a concert pianist, Max is bizarrely good on the tuba.

Joy spoke English with a German accent, Max could do a perfect Colonel Klink after like one *Hogan's Heroes* rerun. Joy painted African wildlife, Max draws Spider-Man. Joy was ten when her parents divorced, which is how old Max was when I finally moved out.

Most of this stuff we discovered together, Max and me hunched at the computer with a couple of Cokes on the go. Last night we read about the time Joy was cajoled into killing a deer (she grew up on the kind of estate where you do that), how horrible it made her feel, how it firmed up her commitment to creatures. They say you forget about your last life when you're still little, so it's no surprise Max doesn't remember this stuff even if he actually is Joy.

But the time I took him fishing? Why doesn't he remember that? It's almost exactly the same as Joy's thing with the deer. We were up on Mabel Lake going for rainbows, and after about four hours we finally got one. As part of his Learning Experience I had Max bash it over the head with a wrench. Like most of my lessons it backfired, didn't toughen him up so much as soften him even further. In a way it's my fault he's so loopy over living things.

Should I remind him about that day, and how it fits with him being Joy? Probably. It's better to have him believing this bunk than even wondering about the truth. I thought I might remind Philomena too, when she called after bedtime tonight to gripe about too much TV (I guess Max got jonesing over there), but I decided against it. I was getting angry again.

"But why not George?" I said.

"What?" Phil wanted to keep talking about the many ways I continue to fail as a father. "Father" always in quotes.

"Why Joy Adamson?" I said. "Why not George, her husband? He's the one who brought Elsa home. He was the real animal guy."

"Yes, but he doesn't feel right," said Phil. "Joy just feels right to me, you know? Max is so gentle, so —"

"He was murdered too," I said. "George Adamson was. Which fits with the reincarnation thing, right? And hey, why is that?"

A weary sigh. I'm always at my worst the day Max moves back to Phil's place, it's a mistake for her to call. "Why is what?"

"Why is it everybody's last life was so dramatic. Everybody was the beheaded queen, nobody was, I don't know. Nobody was the handmaid."

"You were the handmaid, Mark."

I gave her a laugh for that one. That's one thing with me, I can laugh. It's always been bizarre to me that Max can't see what's funny. I said, "And what about karma?"

"Karma?"

Elsie watched me from her usual spot, Max's comfy chair. She was wishing I was smaller so she could kill and eat me. She was thinking, You're a creature too. Don't forget it. "Well, I mean, shouldn't Joy have some good stuff coming? For taking care of Elsa, and all the pain she went through last time? Why would she be reborn to somebody like you?"

A pretty good silence.

I've often tried to picture Max's real dad, the dude Phil cheated with when I was away that one time the year we were married. A gentle giant (Max is almost my size already), musical, creative, crazy about his fellow beings. A little over-serious and slow, like Max. Soft-spoken. I've tried to be more like him, the gentle, life-embracing bit, but not much luck yet. Maybe Max will help me with that one day. "Why would she get reborn," I said, "to a hurter like you?"

Another good silence. Then, "Twelve years, Mark. How long is this going to last?"

And me, "Forever, Phil. Remember?"

Bones

penumbra

I don't know if this is the right place to post this, but I'm stuck. I'm writing a story about the first man, how he lived but mostly how he died. "The Birth of Death" – pretty good, no? The thing is, I'm usually okay at empathizing with my protagonist, but how do I get inside this guy's head? We're talking a million years ago! Help!

aliass

It's about turning off the right side of your brain, the logical side, and waking up the creative side. Maybe go for a walk and look at things, or do some tai chi. I listen to really loud music, mostly nu metal. Check out Touch This.

minimaestro

Start a conversation with your character. Write a question – What's your favourite movie? – except something that fits for a million years ago. Then just let the answer come. Use two different fonts.

blair

Wasn't the first man a woman? Otherwise where did he come from?

opie

Not so sure about your dates, penumbra. The first Homo sapiens lived 250 thousand years ago, and the first member of the genus Homo lived two million years ago. What do you mean "first man"?

zas

Homo is right, lol. Just what we need on this forum, another f**king pedant.

dozer

Put your character in a situation and see what he does. He's sitting there at his campfire and he hears a growl, and it's a saber-toothed tiger. What does he do? Or did they have fire yet?

genjok

The first man is you, and you are the first man. Separation is an illusion, so you have no problem.

opie

Zas, gtfoti.

penumbra

Thanks, minimaestro, that's a great suggestion!

backslash

Yeah, cool title, penumbra! The only thing is, what about everything else that dies? I don't want to be critical – I know how hard it is to get going! – but aren't you being a little anthrocentric? Even carrots die.

opie

It stands for get the f**k off the internet, zas. Which by the way is what you should do if you don't know what it stands for, and even if you do.

rosebud

Hang on, isn't the left side the logical side?

mediumisthemess

You have to find your way in through the details. Think about, what would he have in his pocket? A bone maybe? What type of bone? Or a rock, or a berry, you have to research it and then imagine it. Let those details lead you to the overall sense of who he is. Then figure out how to kill him.

puck

The first humans, if they were humans, to bury themselves were Neanderthals. In the graves with the bones were stone tools and flowers. What tools was your guy good with? But also, you'll need the second man so he can bury the first one. Room for dialogue, if they talked. Did they talk?

zas

Did your mummy never listen to you, opie? Get help man.

penumbra

Good question, dozer. No, they didn't have fire, I just looked it up. I guess that's one of those research details! Btw, great suggestion, mediumisthemess! Thanks!

walserfan

The first human death by robot was thirty-two years ago, at a Ford plant. Just thought you might like to know.

shawnanana

Do a monologue. You're the first man, and you have five minutes to tell us everything important about yourself. Go.

queery

Actually, puck, the first burial goes back to Homo heidelbergensis in Spain, where they found a pink stone ax buried with bones, the first evidence of ritual and symbolic thinking. If that's the first burial, maybe the guy in it is the first man? And maybe pink was his favourite colour? Something to work with.

aliass

You're right, rosebud, sorry. It's left.

carl

The movie Quest for Fire was set eighty thousand years ago and they talked. The language was created by Anthony Burgess, the guy who wrote A Clockwork Orange, and then Stanley Kubrick made a movie of that.

ojo

Right, queery, the first man was a poof and the rest of us came from where? Try making sense lol.

sweetthing

The first man was Adam, and he lived for 930 years (Genesis 5:5). If you mean the first man to die, you mean Abel, who was killed by his brother Cain because God accepted Abel's sacrifice but not Cain's, which wasn't really a sacrifice because it was the fruit of the ground (Genesis 4:3). The first death is a murder. This story has been told, but everyone has their own version. Maybe you should write yours. :)

fallenangle

The first person to die was Lilith, Adam's first wife. She wasn't made out of Adam's body, like Eve was, and she refused to lie under Adam, or any other man, if there were any.

timtime

I'm not trying to be funny, but hasn't death been sort of done to death? From the Bible and Shakespeare, which are full of death, right down to today's news? I'm just saying maybe you should find something new to write about.

kafkask
Lilith is immortal, liu.

writeclick
Glad you weren't trying to be funny, timtime, because you aren't. Or intelligent either. Death is the ONLY subject, except maybe sex (according to Keats, heard of him?). Or are we supposed to stop writing about that too?

crazy242
The wonderful amazing thing about fiction is you make it up for yourself. Just write from your heart!!!

opie
Saber-toothed tigers weren't really tigers at all, but a genus of machairodontine. Not that it's a big deal, but verisimilitude is important if you want people to believe things.

writeclick
I meant Yeats, don't have a frickin' cow.

genjok
Besides which there's no such thing as death. Nothing is ever lost to anything else.

0
Touch This sukz.

◀◀ Previous Thread   Next Thread ▶▶

Anthropocene

The first of the dreams came to Babette early one morning about three years ago. I awoke to the sound of her panting in distress, and I touched her arm.

"What?" she murmured, coming up from under. "Was I ... Oh."

"Bad dream?"

She went up on an elbow and peered about. "There was a ... lion? Yes, big, huge, with a big black mane. It was coming at me. We were in some sort of theatre thing. Stone."

"Ancient Rome? You were a Christian, maybe?" I gave her a dopey chuckle.

"I guess. But I wasn't scared, exactly." She subsided onto her pillow. "I was ... Oh, what a beautiful, strange, beautiful ..."

She was drifting off again. I spoke softly for a while, making up a story about a lion who lived on Christians but longed only for water-lily soup. I fell silent – Babette had commenced gently to snore – without knowing how the story ended.

Later that day I did some research. I'm nerdy that way, and besides, I was between jobs and had time on my hands. Ancient Romans really did throw people to the beasts, I learned, and sometimes those beasts were lions. Barbary lions, to be more precise, imported from North Africa – extra big, with a heavy black mane, just as Babette had described. Which was odd, since there hadn't been Barbary lions for decades.

I shared my discovery with Babette. "It makes you think, doesn't it?" I said. "No shortage of Christians these days." She humoured me for a while, and then lost interest.

A week or so later she recalled another dream. At breakfast one morning she told me how she'd befriended and ridden bareback upon a creature half zebra and half horse. "It was as though the artist ran out of patience part way," she said, closing her eyes as she stirred cream into her coffee. And then, evidently recalling the surge of the dream-creature beneath her, "Such … *power.*"

When she'd left for the office I punched in "half zebra half horse." I expected to discover a rich vein of mythology into which my wife had unconsciously tapped, and I feared that this beast would signify, according to somebody, the sexual vitality that was at that time missing from our bed. Instead I encountered a real animal called a quagga, a subspecies of the plains zebra, half striped and half horse-brown, whose onomatopoeic name (from the language of the Khoikhoi) was said to suggest the animal's guttural call. The last of its kind had died in an Amsterdam zoo in 1883.

I printed off a painting by somebody called Franz Roubal, *The Extermination of the Quagga*. I showed it to Babette when she got home from work that day. She squinted at the fuzzy figures (it was a poor copy), each collapsing in its own balletic fashion. "So you're saying what?" she said.

I shrugged. I was at loose ends. I hoped the next dream would come to me.

A couple of days later Babette asked, "What does an owl sound like?"

I did the *who-who* thing for her.

"So they don't, like, cackle?"

"Not so far as I know."

This time she sat with me while I looked it up. The laughing owl – Babette recognized it from an old black and white photo – was once common in New Zealand. Of the many characterizations of its cry, the best fit for Babette was "a desperate, even demonic laugh." In the dream it apparently laughed at me, though Babette claimed not to recall what I'd done to amuse or horrify it. The last laughing owl was discovered dead on a sheep farm in 1914.

From there the dreams started coming almost nightly. During that first full-on week, Babette was visited by a Honshu wolf, a Bali tiger, a Caribbean monk seal, an ivory-billed woodpecker, a pig-footed bandicoot, a crescent nail-tail wallaby and a Conondale gastric-brooding frog (which opened its mouth wide to show Babette the riot of babies in its gut). All these beasts had died out in something called the Anthropocene, meaning the last couple of hundred years. Carnage-wise, we humans are in the same league as comets and volcanoes, apparently, and have earned our own epoch.

Poor Babette. She started hitting the sack early, waking up and jotting notes during the night. She learned to guide her awareness, ignoring the objects and people that populated her dreams, observing only the animals. Each morning she reviewed her notes with me to assist in my research. Each evening I reported back to her on the newest member of her menagerie.

Why had these creatures chosen my wife's mind as the world in which to be reawakened? Why not mine? How did God pick Noah? It was that sort of thing.

I wanted to go public, of course, still do, but Babette refuses. "I don't know what the point of all this is yet," she'll say, haggard after a particularly haunting night. "What good is it to know what's gone and can't be recovered?" It could make us a fortune, I'll point out, talk shows, book deals – I'm between jobs again, is part of it. But for her that wouldn't be right. This talent isn't personal, but it isn't the opposite either. It's something else.

Babette still does her best work in the wee hours, and that's made our nights eventful. The other morning I awoke four-ish to find her sketching by flashlight, though she soon grew frustrated by her new creature's lack of shape. She'd been swimming with this "big ugly gentle thing," as she put it, a lovable blob that allowed her to stroke it while it grazed on seaweed. "Big ugly gentle thing" – that happens to be how she described me too, back when we were first lovers. On this occasion her thoughts were elsewhere. She spoke with bemused tenderness of the great beast and its hide, "dark and rutty like the bark of some old tree." This was *Hydrodamalis gigas*, as I determined the next day, a school-bus-sized herbivore that once bobbed in the North Pacific. Steller's sea cow, folks called it. It was related to the dugong and the manatee – mermaids in the old myths – which are dying out now too. As a group, they've been around for fifty million years, but they won't be around much longer.

Taking all this in, and recording it as best I can, it strikes me that there are still creatures in existence, some of them almost as fantastic as the ones we've eradicated. Theoretically, a person could go out and be with them. I'm pretty much done with animals by the end of the day, though, and I'm not wild about the company of humans either. I make do with myself and my own benign addictions until Babette gets home. Then I resume the duties of acolyte and scribe.

One upside to Babette's new calling is that she's cut back on the Marlboros and the manhattans, started getting more exercise. She sees it as a duty, what with all the life she'll take with her if she dies – or *when* she dies, I guess would be a more ingenuous way of putting it. As for me, I've at least got something productive-looking to do while I wait for things to open up on the employment front. I identify and catalogue the species, create a little profile for each one. Atlas bear, sea mink, heath hen, blue buck, phantom shiner, rusty numbat, long-billed kaka, black-faced honeycreeper, Hawaiian rail, Tecopa pupfish, Saint Croix racer, Baiji river dolphin, Tasmanian tiger, Formosan clouded leopard, Mariana mallard, Arabian ostrich, Pyrenean ibix, Syrian wild ass, Tokuda's flying fox, Spix's macaw, Cocteau's skink,

Sturdee's pipistrelle, Round Island burrowing boa, broad-faced potoroo, lesser bilby, red-bellied gracile opossum, on and on and on. I love the names – "indefatigable Galapagos mouse" is my current favourite – but most of Babette's creatures (especially the little ones, bugs and such) have never been named, don't exist for us at all. Extra sad, it seems to me, that they died out before they could get themselves discovered. With Babette's help I've roughed out sketches, and I've even started to assign names. There's a red and green newt named after my mum, a stripeless bee named after me. Babette doesn't want an animal of her own, but of course they're all hers.

I wish I could say this new nighttime routine has revived our sex life, but not really. More like replaced it. And I get that – holding all the world's lost creatures in your head must take the pep out of you. Besides which, there's the raw intimacy of it, the natural world opening itself up to her again and again. What need does she have of my big ugly gentle self when she gets to spend the night with a broad-faced potoroo? It's a remarkable gift she's got, and a formidable burden. Her hiding it away makes me wonder what other marvels are out there undiscovered, what else we might not even know we're losing.

The Purpose of Life

"Let's look in on her," I say, buttoning up. "You peed?"

Ken nods.

I flush, fiddle my hands under the tap. "What a day."

"What a day."

Across the hall, Angie's room is illuminated by two night-lights, smears of pale yellow on pink walls. Angie stirs in her crib as we creep in.

"This is what it's all about," I whisper.

Ken touches the small of my back.

"How do you mean, Mummy?" says Angie. From amongst the blankets, the moist glisten of two wide eyes.

"Angie, honey, you should be asleep." I slip a hand under her bottom, come up dry.

"Yes, but what do you mean?" Her bootied feet wave about in the air, blunt antennae. "Tell me and I'll go to sleep." She's been pulling this crap every night since she started talking, which she did at four weeks. *At four weeks*, says the book, *your little darling may coo or burble at you*. At four weeks Angie said "breast," making a big circle with her hands, and then "nipple," making a little one. People tell us not to fret, that each baby is different.

"Well, honey," I say, "I just mean you're what makes it all worthwhile for us. You make it all … make sense."

"That's ridiculous," she says. *Re-dick-all-us* – I love it. "How can *my* life make *your* life make sense? If one life doesn't make sense, how can adding another life to it make it make sense?"

"Hang on," I say. "I'm not saying –"

"Sure you are," says Angie. She squeezes her pudgy fingers into a walnut-sized fist, brandishes it at me. "You're expecting my life to be so replete with meaning that it will assuage your fear of mortality, make up for your own perceived lack of worth. You've failed to justify your own existence, and now you want me to justify my existence and yours too. It's insane, and it's cruel." She mashes her fist into her cheek a few times, finally locates her mouth. She settles in for a good suck.

"But your mummy's right," says Ken. He strokes Angie's silky hair with the backs of his fingers. "You're our purpose, the same way a baby kangaroo is the purpose of a mummy and a daddy kangaroo. The same way a baby polar bear is the purpose of a mummy and a daddy polar bear. The same way –"

Angie pops the gooey fist from her mouth. "But that's so flaccid," she says.

"You mean facile, honey," I say – you get a chance to correct this kid, you grab it. "The word is facile."

Angie's lower lip quivers, a little wet wave reflecting the room's fake moonlight. "Fine, facile," she says, mastering her emotion. "The point is, you're mistaking a necessary condition for a purpose. Reproduction is a necessary condition of life, but does that make it life's purpose? Eating is a necessary condition of life. So is breathing. So is pooping. If we don't poop, life can't go on. Is pooping the purpose of life?"

"There's no need for that kind of talk now, pumpkin," I put in.

"Is the purpose of each thing its own perpetuation?" she persists. "Is the purpose of singing a song to keep on singing it forever?"

"That's a good idea, sweetheart," says Ken. "Let's have a little song, a sleepy song. How about 'Over the Rain —'"

"And anyway," says Angie, "what gives you the idea a living thing should have a purpose? A tool has a purpose. Toilet paper has a purpose. It's for wiping bums."

"That'll be enough of that, young lady," I say.

"But me? I should have a purpose?"

"Peekaboo!" says Ken, popping out from behind his hands.

Angie rolls her eyes. "We're not *for* anything," she says. "I'm not *for* anything."

"Well," I mutter, "at least we know where she got her brains." Ken's too busy peekaboo-ing to rise to this bait. I bend, scoop Angie from her little nest.

"But —"

"Shush," I say.

I ease a breast from under my sweater. She opens her mouth and I fill it.

Hunter

"Dying isn't the worst thing," said the guy. "There are worse things." He did a quick survey of the sleeve of his woolen jacket, found a relatively uncrusty bit and used it to dab at his nose.

"Yeah?"

We were sitting across the aisle from one another on a bus headed south, which for me meant home. I wasn't hung over. He wasn't either so far as I could tell, but we were both stupefied by a night spent dealing with the unwieldiness of our own bodies. Unwieldiness? Something like that, something to hint at the disjunction between our bodies and the space provided for them on the bus, and beyond that, at the basic discomfort and uncanniness of physical life. Plus we were a little shaken by what had just happened, or almost happened.

"Yeah," said the guy. "Living when you should have died, that's worse." I figured he was twice my age, fiftyish. Recent years did not appear to have been easy on him. "That's way worse."

"Really? You think so?"

"I know so."

A few minutes back, the bus had braked hard and swerved for something on the highway. One person up front said dog, another said deer. We slammed into the guardrail and shrieked along it for a bunch of seconds, long enough for each of us to contemplate something that wouldn't happen if we went over and were crushed and incinerated. I wouldn't get to see Andrea, for instance, who was waiting for me at the other end.

The guy shook his head, made a humourless little chuckling sound. "Is Jake miserable?" he said. "Is Monty?"

"Jake?" I said.

"Or Monty."

"I'm guessing no?" It wasn't just us, everybody was chatting now, one stranger to another. You couldn't help it once you'd come that close.

"No," said the guy. "You can't be miserable if you're dead. You can be one or the other, but you can't be both."

I was on my way back from school after my final exams. They'd gone well, though "Islamic Art from the Mongol Conquests to the Dawn of the Modern Period" had been brutal. The point being, I now possessed a bachelor's degree in this and that. A death of sorts, like any accomplishment. The end of something. I knew it, but I didn't know quite how to feel about it yet, beyond the slightly sickening anxiety I felt about everything in those days.

And now Andrea. We'd dated in high school, separated to go to different universities, then hooked up again online. We'd been having remote sex over the last few months, each of us masturbating in front of a laptop. I could open my eyes and watch her watching me while she went at it alone, or I could close my eyes and remember us going at it together a few years back, in her parents' TV room, my parents' Toyota. It had become a thing with us, a way of overcoming the weirdness of the physical distance, that we'd always come together, that neither of us would ever be left alone. So I had to take my time, distract myself with some little worry. What would become of us when we were together again in the flesh? That sort of thing.

"In the Ilkhanid period," I said, "there was a great cultural flowering."

"What?" said the guy.

"Almost sort of growing out of the devastation of the Mongol conquests. Beautiful textiles and pottery and everything. And books."

"So?"

"A good thing out of a bad thing."

He had another go at staunching his nose. It occurred to me that he might have been crying on the sly over there.

"I guess what I'm getting at is, sometimes you just have to leave stuff behind. Move on."

"Wise man, are you?" He looked at me over his glasses, then through them, then over them, as though the distance between us was wrong no matter what.

"Not wise," I said, snorting a laugh, "just … I'm sorry."

"We should've died, you and me," he said.

"Pardon?"

"Why do I keep on not dying?"

I tried but failed to come up with a useful answer to this question. We fell silent, as everybody else was starting to do too. I should perhaps have been preoccupied with my own mortality, but instead got wondering about Jake and Monty, what might have happened to them that didn't happen to my friend. I've wondered about it ever since. Well, obviously not, but it's something I do ponder when my mind returns to that day, five years ago. Five years, long enough for Andrea and me to break up, get back together, get married, have Sky, and break up again. It's a form of regret, the pondering – regret that I didn't ask the guy, didn't have the nerve to go further into his trauma with him. His *survivor's guilt* – I've searched it, and it rings true for me. I see it in the faces of friends these days, friends whose marriages have endured, who wake up with lovers and little kids nearby. I don't know exactly what happens when they look at me, but something does.

For a while I was thinking Vietnam – I'd detected a bit of an American accent, something southern. Jake, Monty, and my guy (why didn't I get his name?) had served as tunnel rats in Cu Chi or someplace, Jake and Monty blown up by a booby trap while my guy was around the corner taking a leak. But then it occurred to me, that doesn't even work if he's fifty, the dates are wrong. So I switched to a hunting accident. In my mind the three of them putter across a lake in Jake's flat-bottomed boat. The deer are over yonder. Somebody gets silly, the boat gets rocking and flips. Two guys go down – they're more heavily laden with gear, perhaps – and my guy's left bobbing there alone. A big buck stops and sniffs the air, melts back into the woods.

I told Andrea about it once, about how I almost died on my way to her that day (I kept it to myself at the time, as I was keeping a lot of things), about the man I met, and the story I dreamt up to explain his despair. What she got fixated on, for some reason, was his theory about the afterlife.

"Why not?" she said. "Why couldn't you be both miserable and dead?"

"Or joyous," I said. "Why couldn't you be both joyous and dead?" She was pregnant with Sky at the time, and I was pressing her to have cheery thoughts. I believed it might make a difference, predispose Sky to a happy life. Me trying to manipulate her, was how Andrea interpreted it, as she was interpreting more and more of my behaviour at the time. "You can't *control* me," she'd say.

And of course she was right. What I can control, I realize, is nothing. I don't know why this lifts my spirits, but it does.

Ex

Dear Sam,

I'm not the person to write this letter, I know that. Go ahead and curse me out, okay? Get it over with. Then read on.

First off, a bit of news. I've left Larry again. For good this time. Does that make things better for you, or even worse? Any chance you two might be friends again? Not best friends, but then I'm not convinced you ever were. That was for effect, wasn't it? "She left me for my friend" is okay, but "She left me for my *best* friend" has so much more oomph. It's an art form with you, fashioning the dreary into the dramatic.

Anyhow, I thought you'd want to know. Larry says Lynne says your novel is about a novelist and a filmmaker, about you and me. I'm not sure how far you're going, chronologically, but it's a different outcome, I would think, if the unfaithful one also ends up alone. A different arc. Maybe you'll want to leave the me-character remarried, though. Benightedly content in her bourgeois enslavement, the bitch.

You know I think of myself that way too, right? You know I hate myself as much as you do?

Larry says Lynne says you're only a little way into the novel, but that it's going to be really good. "Scary good" is how she describes it. She's generally more tactful than that with Larry (it must have been tricky at times, representing the two of you, especially when you were both schtupping her), so she's obviously knocked out. For which, congratulations.

But you've got to stop. This is not a book you should write.

Again, I'm the wrong person to make the argument. There's clearly self-interest involved. Do I want to read your version of me? Do I want others to read it? I don't.

But my self-interest goes beyond that, and it dovetails with yours. What's good for me is, this one time, good for you too. Larry says Lynne says the novel's going to be in three parts, structured around your three attempts to kill yourself after I left. Brain. Breath. Blood. It's smart, but it's also suicidal. If you spend too much time with this stuff, if you go back inside it, how will you ever get out again?

You hate it when I obsess about the holocaust (or at least you used to, it's not likely you care one way or the other anymore), but it's my personal history, sort of, and I can't see deleting it from my life, or from my work, or from my way of thinking about things. Anyhow, I want to talk about survivors. What they tend to do is survive, right? Not just survive but (look at Bubby) thrive. They get married, they have kids. They build things, they contribute to things. They live, and their lives are a great big Bronx cheer to death and its side-kicks. What they don't do is kill themselves. What they don't do is capitulate.

But then look at Primo Levi. Look at Paul Celan. Look at Bruno Bettelheim. I don't have to go on, do I? Okay, then look at Jean Amery, Jerzy Kosinski, Tadeusz Borowski, Piotr Rawicz ... All holocaust writers who killed themselves, of course. The parallel is preposterous, maybe even repugnant, but do you see my point? It wasn't the holocaust part that killed them, it was the writing part. They were just like the other survivors, except they kept trying to articulate what had happened. They re-entered the trauma in order to reveal it to us.

You'll go back. You'll write a good book. It may be helpful to others, but it won't help you. When you say, "They were soused and savaging each other daily" (that line is yours, if you like), it won't make it any less true. When you say, "She came at him with a paring knife," it won't mean I didn't do it, it'll mean I'm doing it again. Just let it stop.

I got the green light on the Primo Levi project, by the way, the one I talked about way back when. The idea that his death wasn't a suicide at all but just an accident? You said suicide was an accident too. You said everything's an accident. We didn't fight about it, imagine!

Rach

Customer Review

The Sinking Lifeboat: How Death Could Save Us [Hardcover]
<u>R.L. Clark</u> (Author)

2 of 3 people found the following review helpful

★★★☆☆ Worth losing sleep over
By G. Bailey (Vancouver, Canada) – <u>See all my reviews</u>

If you want to freak yourself out sometime, like I just did, have a look at the world population clock. There are going on eight billion people right now, all thinking thoughts and going to the bathroom and so on, eight *billion*, and that goes up by another eighty million per year. That's like adding another Iran every year, though of course not everybody being born is a Muslim. Not that I have anything against Muslims, except the batty ones but that goes for everybody. Anyhow, there are four people born every second and only two die, and that's what this book is about: death, which we need more of. Nobody seems to have heard of this book, which isn't surprising because nobody wants to think about it, but poverty and starvation and ruining the environment are going to keep getting worse unless we do. Think about dying, that is, and actually die.

One unique thing about this book is that he talks about not just human rights but also animal rights. We're basically infesting the planet, which you can't deny. But what we do deny is death. We live in denial, says R.L. Clark, which is why we impose ourselves on the world, trying to make ourselves big with power and possessions and fancy ideas (like this one, guilty!), and also why we insist on surviving no matter what. Only if we accept death can we make life possible for all living creatures, even the ones that bother us.

Maybe the best thing about this book is that the author doesn't tell you he's dying until the last chapter. He has something called "fatal familial insomnia" which is basically that you can't sleep, and you lose your mind and fall apart. Maybe that's why he can talk about all this, not just because he's dying but because he can't sleep. Actually he can sleep for now, the disease hasn't hit him yet, but it will, and that must make it hard to sleep. The only thing is, there's no cure for his disease. If there was a cure, would he really not take it? Are we supposed to believe he'd stay awake when he could be sleeping instead of dead, though in some ways what's the difference?

Plus there's a big thing he's missing and that's, sorry guys, but feminism. If women had control of their bodies they wouldn't choose to be pregnant all the time. I've read that one in five pregnancies in the world isn't wanted by the woman, or it might even be two in five. Full disclosure: my wife is pregnant right now, with our second, both of which we agreed on. But if women all over the world had power, so they only had the children they wanted, you'd cut down most of the overpopulation, or a lot of it anyway. Then just a bit more death and we'd be okay.

Also, it's rich people who have to start kicking the bucket (though euphemisms are part of the problem according to R.L. Clark). We can't count on the people who're dying in Africa and places like that because they don't eat much, and have puny little carbon footprints. It's people like you and me who have to snuff it, and I hope we do for the sake of Liam, and either Ryder or Rebecca, though not till they're older.

Was this review helpful to you? Yes ☐ No ☐ **Report Abuse**

Extras

This story, their story, will be even better when they're old.
They'll tell it to friends, and to strangers. They'll tell it to
their kids so often there'll be talk of dementia. They'll tell it
to one another, tossing in fresh details to enhance each new
rendition.

"I had a scar over this eye," Jacques will say. "Running
all the way down to my chin." He'll inscribe the swoop of it
with the tip of a finger.

"And a flap of flesh just here," Oriana will say, pressing a
palm to his temple, which by then will be grey.

"Your left eye dangled halfway down your cheek," he'll say,
"and there were streaks of blood on your cheerleader's skirt.
They were random, but not random."

"Right."

They'd both auditioned, but on different days, so they
didn't see one another until they were no longer themselves.

They were both skinny, and pretty good at moaning and shambling and tipping over when somebody impaled them or shot them in the head, so they made it into group A, the group that would be closest to the camera. That meant hours in the makeup artist's chair. By the time they met they were dramatically altered.

"How did we recognize one another?" they'll marvel. "How did we know, under all the guck?"

They each had their own reason for responding to the ad. Oriana happened to be working on an article for a pop culture magazine, her very first sale. Her topic was cosmetic surgery, specifically the botched surgery of a young movie star. Oriana came at it through the undead. "Our most fundamental terror," she wrote, "is that we might turn out to be objects. We aren't afraid of being transformed into zombies, we're afraid we *are* zombies. Zombies with good manners, our guts neatly sausaged inside our skins." After many years, she'll still recall the thrill these sentences gave her as they composed themselves on the page. "A zombie longs to eat us, the same way a rock longs to roll down a hill. What if our desires, too, are just impersonal laws being worked out on our bodies?" Then she segued to the surgery. "A surgically altered face is disturbing in the same way a zombie is disturbing. The starlet wants to transcend her limited physicality, but in fact she affirms it for herself, and for us. We watch her turn into a thing." The piece needed one more dimension, an element of vulnerability or risk on the author's part. Signing on as an extra in a zombie series? Perfect.

Whereas Jacques just liked to be scared. How could that be? How could a bad thing be a good thing? Maybe he'd figure it out on set.

For the first day's scene they were assigned – after hours of sitting around, shyly grinning at one another through their gore – to a mob of zombies hunting a pregnant woman. It was a happy episode – the pregnant woman decapitated them all with a broadsword she'd fashioned from a length of rusty gutter. The only person they overtook and ate was a sleaze-ball who'd tried to sacrifice everybody to save himself.

"You were so good," Jacques will recall. "You really tucked into that jerk!"

"You too," Oriana will say. "I completely bought everything you did. Remember that moan you had going?"

"And how you kept slinging your eye out of the way while you chowed down?" Jacques will mime this maneuver, a fashion model's hair flip.

"We were gruesome."

"We were gruesome."

She'll pause a moment, get wistful. "That was the first time we touched. Remember?"

"Of course. We jostled each other as we tried to get at the good bits."

"You had his brains all to yourself. But then –"

"I let you in," he'll say.

"You let me in."

And so on. They'll just keep summoning details like this, conjuring up the moment of their meeting. They'll do this more and more often over the years, and never tire of it.

Without the need to say so, they'll share the view that starting out undead made them immortal, that death had touched
them and let them go. Nothing will ever rob them of this belief.

Squirrel

My journal prompt from Ms. Lopez who is our sub until Mr. Kisch finishes his breakdown is What do you believe in? I don't know is too short since this has to be 250 words. I'm writing on my spiral notepad with Mum's phone as a flashlight in the passenger seat. The dashboard bobblehead of Albert Einstein who was a bad student Mum says to make me feel better and didn't wear socks is nodding. My sister is asleep in the back seat, we take turns. Mum is trying to sleep in the driver's seat because she has to get up early to go behind the bakery for buns. We're supposed to use details so this is a 1998 Ford Escape which was my aunt's. Ford means to cross something and escape obviously means escape. I'm not supposed to touch dead animals, no one is, which is why I can't tell Mum although I suppose she might read this. For details the squirrel was grey and soft and cold like the pavement.

When I picked him up he stayed the same with his hands up to his face. Squirrel is a strange word when you stop and think about it. I held him for a while and then chucked him into the bushes at the edge of the church parking lot where we park every other night. The church doesn't look like a church, just a building that goes up a bit over the door. I tried to find him again in the bushes but couldn't. I thought maybe he was alive and ran away but that doesn't make sense. Mum is snoring now which is good because she's asleep and also I sleep better when she snores which also doesn't make sense. Since I picked up the squirrel I see light in people's heads. Maybe I always did and didn't notice. Now I get hot and people's heads turn colours like purple for Ms. Lopez. The light mostly stays in her head but sometimes comes out a bit. My sister Tree just said either puzzle or nuzzle in her sleep, or some other word that rhymes with them. The light in my sister's head is red but the light in my mother's head is almost more like green or sometimes blue. In the mirror after we shower at the Y the light in my head is no color, there's something wrong with me but no one else can see it. What does believing something mean? I believe the squirrel ran away or do I only hope so? That's enough words probably but my fingers are too cold outside my sleeping bag to count them. To be safe another detail is Ms. Lopez thinks I'm the class clown but I only am since she said so. I like that people like my squirrel noises but I also like Ms. Lopez. If this isn't enough words sorry.

Angel, Still Ugly

People can't seem to agree on which of Vincent Van Gogh's paintings was his last. Most poetic would be *Wheatfield with Crows*, since it was in a wheat field that he subsequently shot himself in the chest, but it could just as easily have been *Daubigny's Garden* or *Tree Roots and Trunks* or even *Thatched Sandstone Cottages in Chaponval*.

In the case of Paul Klee it was most likely *Still Life* (which is poetic too, or ironic or something), a painting that contains a kettle and a moon and also a sheet of paper on which is sketched another of his late works, *Angel, Still Ugly*, by which he seems to have meant an angel who hasn't yet risen all the way from carnality to spirituality. If I were an artist, and if I believed there to be a difference between carnality and spirituality, and if that title weren't taken, I might grab it.

Today is the second anniversary of my son's death. Some days I say "my son's suicide," some days I don't. My wife, before she left me last year, told me it was time to stop laying blame. She said the same thing again when she came back earlier this month. It's odd, because I'm not aware of having blamed anybody. When exactly did we stop comprehending one another?

Van Gogh and Klee both had a tough time. With Van Gogh it was simple despair, if that's the right word to describe somebody who eats his paint. In Klee's case it was physical pain, a type of sclerosis that attacked his whole body, including his skin, so that his face hardened into a mask of itself. One of these artists killed himself, the other did not. "The longing for death," Klee wrote in his diary, "not as destruction, but as striving toward perfection." He kept producing, a thousand works in his final year, until the illness caused the brush to fall from his hand.

So there's a choice. You can stop or you can keep going. My son seems to have made one choice, I seem to have made the other. I'm tempted to think he was in the right, but perhaps I'm in the right too. Knowing I can kill myself, perhaps I don't need to? In this sense my son saved me, made my suicide unnecessary by showing me it was possible, if that's actually what he did. I'd rather it had been the other way around, I'd give anything to switch destinies with him, but this desire of mine appears to have no bearing on anything whatsoever.

My wife comes to bed tonight, a slash of magenta across her forehead. I shut out the light and we lie side by side in the mottled darkness.

"Any luck?" I ask. She's back in her studio for the first time since our son's death. I have the impression the ideas aren't flowing.

"Not sure," she says.

Like me, our son was not artistic. What he had the knack for was making things work. He took things apart and put them together again.

"There's a new theory," I say. "About Van Gogh. That he didn't actually kill himself."

"Oh?"

"That it was a schoolboy who shot him. By mistake."

My wife is silent.

"He'd just ordered paints. He'd sent a relatively upbeat letter to his brother. There was no suicide note."

In our son's case, too, there was no note. His girlfriend discovered him stretched out in their backyard where he'd apparently been gazing up at the stars, or at the clouds behind which there would have been stars. In the bathroom she found empty bottles of his painkillers and his antidepressants. Even assuming the bottles were full to begin with, it shouldn't have been enough. Surely he would have known this.

My wife says, "I'm trying to paint him. From that photo, him coming through the door, sort of looking up and to his left? In his little blazer?"

"On 6th Avenue."

"I think it was Frances Street."

"Not 6th?"

"I don't think so."

I turn as though to look at her, the spot she occupies in the dark. "You have a smear of something on your forehead. Magenta, I think."

"Yes. Well, violet."

"What will it be?" Violet hair. Violet eyes. Violet.

"I don't think I can do it," she says.

I open my mouth. I make a sound. We both cry for a bit, and then we make love.

Once my wife is asleep I get up and creep downstairs. Out in the backyard it's raining, and then it stops. That things can still be beautiful.

Machu Picchu

She'd never regret the things she did, only the things she didn't do – of this she was assured many times, back when she was alive. The people who offered up this nugget of wisdom were generally selling her something, or pushing some other agenda of their own. They'd deliver it in the world-weary tone of those who bear the burden of being right, but they were wrong.

She regrets so many things she did. She regrets, for instance, the night she agreed to go out dancing with a former student to a place known for something called deep micro house music, a stripped-down, thumpy, pulsating sort of thing that made her intensely euphoric, so much so that she let the young man kiss and caress her on the dance floor despite the fact that he was far too young and not especially gifted. There was nothing terribly regrettable about this, and indeed the long walk afterwards, during which he spoke with fervour about matriarchy in the Neolithic age and other diverting subjects, was rather sweet. But when she got home in the wee hours she discovered her dog Arvo having some kind of fit on the kitchen floor, unable to rise yet going at a full gallop, driving his head again and again into the base of the stainless steel fridge. She pinned him down while he died, then began to bawl in a way that made her believe she'd never stop. She did stop, but this only intensified her pain.

And really, what an idiotic idea. How could you distinguish between things you did and things you didn't do? How was doing something not also not doing something? If you went out dancing, you didn't stay home with your dog. If you stayed home with your dog, you didn't go out dancing. If you spent your first honeymoon (that whole first marriage was a poor idea) in Peru sampling piranha as served in various cities, in Lima and in Huaraz and in Trujillo, you didn't spend it walking the Inca trail to Machu Picchu. Saying yes was saying no, and vice versa. Yes and no were indistinguishable, because you were always saying both.

So there's nothing to stop her regretting the things she did as well as the things she didn't do. This is what she does. She regrets the bad things she did, and she regrets the good things she didn't do. She regrets spending so much of her shortish life dividing things up into bad and good, and she regrets the fact that she still does this, here in this exhausting afterlife with its stringent, almost mean-spirited diet and its onerous exercise regimen. Is this program for everybody, or just for her? Is it meant to punish her for something she's done, or to prepare her for something she has yet to do? How is it that she's still so bewildered?

There's no way to know if she'll get another life — it seems a long shot, what with the state of planet earth when she quit it — but she's making plans just in case. Next time she'll do exactly the other thing. She'll drop money into every upturned hat, what the hell. She'll lavish such vigilant care on the creatures around her that they'll glow with received reverence. She'll make it to Machu Picchu and pray alone to nobody in the Temple of the Sun. She'll do the things she didn't do and undo the things she did, so that when she dies next time it will be for good.

Crepuscular

It was odd, Lucy leaving him the fish. They weren't much more than acquaintances, he and Lucy. They'd both signed up for over-fifty ping pong at about the same time, almost a year ago now, and they were both beginners with no natural ability, so they did tend to get paired up. And Dennis did have more patience with her than some of the other players. Lucy was inclined to quote great thinkers, loudly and in ludicrous contexts. Flubbing a serve one time she hollered, "Well, you know Hegel, *The mystery is is, the mystery is was.*" Not much chance that this was actually Hegel, or anybody else for that matter, but so what? Dennis readied himself to jot the gem down on an invisible pad, and Lucy, laughing, repeated it almost verbatim.

It seemed slight grounds upon which to write a person into your will, though. Plus Dennis was older than Lucy, and in dodgier health. If anything, he should have been leaving stuff to her. Plus there were no fish.

Lucy's nephew read the relevant bit of the will over the phone. "To Dennis at ping pong I leave my guppies, Joan and Miró, and all their issue."

"I don't understand," said Dennis.

"But I've got the right Dennis? From ping pong?"

"Yes. But I'm not sure … why would she leave me her guppies?"

"She didn't. I mean, she did, but she hasn't got any guppies. Or any other fish, as far as I've been able to determine. Did the two of you … was there ever any talk of fish?"

"Not as I recall."

Lucy's nephew gave a rueful chuckle. He urged Dennis not to fret about the whole business. "This isn't even the weirdest part," he said. "Hey, by the way, before I let you go, Lucy never mentioned the … Cuchiyaku people of Ecuador, did she?"

"I don't believe so, no."

Lucy's nephew thanked him, apologized that the bequest had come to nothing, and hung up.

There was a Joan Miró painting called *Singing Fish*. Even on Dennis's computer screen it was exquisite, a delicate shattering of shape and colour. At first you didn't see the fish because it swam not horizontally but vertically, rising up out of some depth. Towards what? Was it a message, a metaphor?

Or maybe it was just that Lucy perceived Dennis as lonely. Retired, widowered, kids abroad and busy with their lives. Perhaps she imagined pets would perk him up.

The guppies at the store were fancier than the ones Dennis had pictured. They sported great vivid tails that rippled like medieval banners. As a boy, Dennis had inherited an aquarium and its fish from a friend who'd had to move away with his family. There were no guppies, only an angelfish that promptly died, and a pair of neon tetras, little zaps of red and blue light. Dennis had every intention of naming them, but failed to come up with names that weren't depressingly obvious. Then one morning there were a bunch of tiny, transparent babies flitting about the aquarium. Dennis told everybody at school, and a few kids rode home with him at lunch to check them out. The babies were gone, eaten by their parents. The parents died too, soon enough. Dennis could no longer remember to feed them.

The pet store also carried rodents. A chubby, squirrel-sized creature caught Dennis's eye, a sort of cross between a rabbit and a mouse. "Native to South America," read a handwritten sign, "the Chinchilla is smart, clean, and incredibly soft. Crepuscular, meaning most active at dusk and dawn. A great jumper!"

"Sweet, eh?" A young woman looked up from a display of catnip toys she was arranging.

"Crepuscular," said Dennis. "I didn't know that word. I'm that too. Crepuscular."

"Cool," said the young woman. She wore a T-shirt that read, "Stop eating meat and I'll show you my breasts."

"I'm not much of a jumper, though," said Dennis.

The young woman smiled. "Me neither." Judging by her athletic appearance, this was a fib.

"I'll take her," said Dennis.

"Cha-cha? That's what we call her, but of course you can call her whatever you like."

"Here we go again," said Dennis.

"Pardon me?"

"Hegel. I'll call her Hegel." She'd die too, of course, but this was hardly her fault.

"Awesome," said the young woman. She stood and started ticking items off on her fingers. "Cage. Water bottle. Dust for her to bathe in."

"Dust?"

The young woman nodded. "You won't believe how happy it'll make her."

Homeward bound, Hegel chattering from her cage on the passenger seat like a sat-on squeeze toy, Dennis thought to himself, Happy. He thought, Happy.

Welcome

By the time you read this I'll still be alive. You'll get home
from your mum's place, you'll push through the door with
your little red rolly overnight bag and call out, "Babe?" Silence.
You'll spot this note on the table and sit down to read it, I'm
guessing, without even plucking off your wool hat with the
dangly things, so silly it's cool. And you'll get mad at me again,
but not as mad as you'd have been if I'd written the other note.

The other note would have been a playlist, mostly. Music
for my funeral. The playlist would have been my will, too. The
songs would have been my gifts, behests I think they're called,
since I don't have anything else to leave behind. Except the
speakers, which we bought together so of course they'd have
been yours. Oh, and my bike. You'd probably have given it to
Nick, since it's too big for you, plus you don't like orange. Why
is that? I think I asked you once, but did you tell me? Don't
forget that orange is the colour of basketballs and Cheezies
and flames, depending on what's burning.

It was hard nailing down the list, but for some reason it's got me feeling a little less like crap. Two full days I spent, almost half your cooling off time, assuming you actually do come home today. Fingers crossed. Should the songs relate to me, or to suicide, or to the people I was dedicating them to, or what? I started with Baby's On Fire, which was for Nick but of course it's me who's obsessed with it. If I was going to choose a Brian Eno it should have been something soft and ambient, obviously, so people could be somber, but the Robert Fripp solo – well, you've caught me air guitaring to it a few times, so you know. For Mum I went Hallelujah, the k.d. lang one, not because I'm crazy about it (I'm actually kind of meh) but because Mum would be hurt if nobody cried (I choked up pretty good just thinking about her listening to it, to tell you the truth). For Dad I went Violent Femmes because that would mystify him, and for Maya I went Bach (Italian Concerto, Glenn Gould) because that would mystify her. For you I was thinking, maybe you'll hate this, but I was thinking 4'33", John Cage. My idea was that you'd perform it yourself, go up to the piano or probably organ (Dad would insist on the church) and just sit there for four and a half minutes letting everybody listen to themselves and the world. Because it's all music, of course, which in a way is what I've realized while you've been gone.

The thing about killing yourself, other than it's brutal for everybody else, is it doesn't solve the problem. The problem is being born, the opposite of which isn't dying. When you die you're still you, you're just dead, right? What you have to become isn't dead, but whatever the actual opposite of born is.

Not so easy, but for sure you have to be alive to even try. You can't stop having the stuff you got by being born, but maybe you can stop it being yours, give it back to nature by watching yourself, a naturalist. Which is what I'm doing right now, noticing this thought as it emerges from me like some sort of, I don't know. Like blood from a cut. It is what it is, just like everything else.

Yeah, I found your private stash (you really didn't think I'd rummage through your tampons?), but that's not what's going on here. These aren't the kind of insights that turn out to be idiocy when you come down the next day. It's already the next day, so I'd know.

Why am I telling you all this? Because that's what we're doing from now on, we're telling each other stuff. Sure, I might still be lying. I might not have thought about killing myself, or I might have thought about it and decided to go ahead. I might be dead right now, the right now of you reading this. Once a guy's lied to you (it was three times with Mari, by the way, not two like I told you the other day, but one of us really did cry after each time, her twice and me once), why would you believe him when he says he's stopped lying? Why wouldn't that be a lie too?

Beats me. You know that thing where you say "this is a lie"? Which if it's true it's false and if it's false it's true? Maybe this is like that. Or okay, maybe not.

It's about noon right now, the right now of me writing this. The right now of you reading this is probably late afternoon. I'm heading over to Nick's to give you time. I've taken my toothbrush, and I'll wait for you to call. I'll wait as long as I have to. I'll wait forever, though that's obviously an exaggeration, which is a lie, so pretend I didn't write it.

I know you've been worried about me, especially with my mother and everything, but to tell you the truth I've kind of been milking that. Having a mother who tried to kill herself isn't at all the same as having one who did. And I'm sorry if this note spooked you again, but you can stop worrying. I don't think I'd ever off myself even if there was a point, which there isn't. Like I say, if I was dead I'd still just be me, whereas I'm already different. I wouldn't write this note, would I?

Oh, and for Yash I was going to go John Coltrane, that song Welcome, the one that sounds like Happy Birthday. You pointed that out to me one time, right? We were on a train going someplace, sharing my headphones, one bud each. It'd be funny, or maybe the word is ironic, what with me lying there all dead. Plus of course it's beautiful beyond belief, like you, like everything. Like you.

Welcome. Call me when you're ready to, okay? There's still half a joint in the tampon box. In the fridge there's salad and quinoa and one of those samosas.

the end of me

Acknowledgments

I'd like to express my gratitude to the fine people at Freehand Books for embracing this project: Kelsey Attard, Anna Boyar, the members of the editorial board, and especially Deborah Willis, my kind and clear-eyed editor. Also to Cap'n Bill Gaston, whose attentive readings have helped me navigate some tricky fictional waters, and to the other esteemed members of the GFC: Jay Connolly, Jay Ruzesky, Bill Stenson and Terence Young. Sara Cassidy and Julie Paul offered insight and encouragement; Celso Cambiazo and Pierre Mackenzie helped me with translations; Leslie McGarry provided valuable feedback. Learning of the theme of this book, people often directed promising leads my way – I'll single out Sylvia Weinstock, and there have been many others.

My parents, who died while I was at work on these stories, are a constant, guiding presence for me. My kids – I include my own two, as well as my niece and her partner, my nephew, and my daughter-in-law, adding a shout-out to little Isadora – are always there to inspire me even when they don't happen to be nearby. My brothers-in-law are my brothers (plus one!). My sister, Anne Louise Gould, and my wife, Sandy Mayzel, offered wise counsel regarding this work, and have supported me in this as in all my endeavours. These people are the greatest blessings of my very fortunate life.

I'm thankful for the many friends, colleagues and students who've helped animate and shape my relationship with thinking and writing over the years. And I'm thankful to have the opportunity to live and work in this magnificent place, at the southern tip of Vancouver Island, on the unceded territory of the Lekwungen (Songhees and Esquimalt) people.

My thanks to the Canada Council for the Arts and the British Columbia Arts Council for financial assistance during the writing of this book. Also to Douglas Glover and the editors of *Numero Cinq*, who previously published some of these pieces.

Thanks finally to Natalie Olsen of Kisscut Design, for the gorgeous cover and book design.

It isn't possible to acknowledge all the other works that have informed this one, but I'll mention (without, of course, holding responsible) a few. For "Via Negativa" I'm indebted to Dr. Emma Bryne, *Swearing Is Good for You*; for "Pulse" to Yoel Hoffmann, editor of *Japanese Death Poems*; for "The Rule and Exercises of Holy Dying" to cleric Jeremy Taylor who authored the original work of that title; for "The Works" to "The Gospel of Thomas" in the *Nag Hammadi Library*; for "From the Journal of Dr. Duncan MacDougall of Haverhill, Mass." to Dr. Duncan MacDougall and his "Hypothesis Concerning Soul Substance Together with Experimental Evidence of the Existence of Such Substance"; for "Party Game" to mystic Douglas Harding, *On Having No Head*; for "About Me" to philosopher and poet Jan Zwicky, *Plato as Artist*; for "Shrub" to philosopher Derek Parfit, *Reasons and Persons*; for "Stage" to Ruth Davis Konigsberg, *The Truth About Grief.*